AF295280

*Diary of
a fallen so(u)ldier*

*Diary of
a fallen so(u)ldier*

Sebastian Blasco

NORBODA

Norboda © 1442/2021, Lund

Originaltitel: Diary of A Fallen So(u)ldier

Författare: Sebastian Abdul-Salaam Blasco

Omslagsfoto: Max Stockman

Formgivning och sättning: Helena Wikström

Tryck: BoD - Books on Demand, Norderstedt, Tyskland

ISBN: 978-91-9850-119-3

The following was found in three notebooks in Syria about four years ago. I struggled with the decision whether to publish it or not due to the highly personal character of the content, the fact that I never got to meet the author and also the fact that it wasn't mine to begin with. After reading the diary countless times I came to the conclusion that it was not a choice, but rather incumbent upon me to make an effort for the words contained therein to reach as many people as possible. This due to the presumed desire of the original author to share his story for mankind to learn lessons from it and him wanting to reach out to his mother and brother, who could not be located by myself or anyone whose help I sought in that endeavour. Perhaps someone that knows her and will recognize her son in the pages that follow will alert her to her child's last words that are partially directed to the one that brought him into this world. I don't know the author or anything about him at all except for what he tells us himself in his diary. He signed it with a few different names but they are not enough to establish his identity. His death is certain beyond any doubt in my opinion. I have reached this conclusion after doing research on the location where the notebooks were found and having it confirmed by multiple independent sources that the platoon fighting in that same region was completely wiped out, not a single survivor. I came to learn that the squadron that the writer was a part of got split up into smaller groups, which is also confirmed by the author himself in his writing, and there were no prisoners taken and no one was able to escape.

Reporters were allowed in the region a few months after it had been secured and fighting had ceased. For reporting purposes we were free to move in the area and document under the supervision of the group that was controlling that part of Syria at the time. The different factions that defeated the army that the author was a part of had taken all the spoils that they wanted and needed upon defeating their foe. A lot of footage was taken and the very few items that were left after the spoils had been picked up and distributed were there for the taking. There was not much at all for us to claim. Some torn clothes, old canisters, a variety of different shells and a lot of insignificant warfare paraphernalia. We looked in all the houses, they looked like what you would expect abandoned houses to look like, except they were even more barren than you would expect. Not a single edible item, running water was a distant memory in this part of Syria. Not a thing of value seemed to remain. Not even pictures left behind as these are very valuable commodities for smugglers. We were looking for anything of value to a reporter. Anything that could be a part of a feature and be an interesting anecdote in a story. There was not much to grasp at. As I was standing in what must have been a temporary bedroom, I wanted to move the blanket from the mattress to see if there was anything underneath, but instead I felt something wrapped in the blanket. Perhaps in a last effort to safeguard his memoirs the fallen soldier made an attempt to preserve his last words before his fall. Wrapped in the blanket I found three notebooks that I at first did not think that much of except that it was uplifting to at least find something that might be of interest after searching for so long. As I later on started looking in them I realized it wasn't your run-of-the-mill notebooks with some phone numbers in it, a couple of to do lists and some doodling. It was a diary that ended at about the same date that the conflict in this very area had ended. I soon came to the realization that what I had found was not curiosities to be used as a side note in some bigger story, rather what I had found was the actual story itself.

I have tried not to edit the text more than what was necessary. It was handwritten in what I consider fairly good handwriting, though extremely small, as he had made a concerted effort to fit as many words as possible on each page. I did correct a few grammatical and a few spelling errors. I have chosen to italicize words that the author had underlined for emphasis. I did this to stay true to traditional literary convention. Overall I think it was well-written. The errors are easily forgiven considering that they were written under very tough circumstances as there was a war raging and the author was on the run trying to extend his lifespan. Other than correcting the few linguistic errors I have not tampered with the text whatsoever in order not to distort the message that the author wanted to send out. At various places the handwriting was hard to decipher. Sometimes due to occasional sloppiness in the handwriting and at other times due to the letters being corrupted by what I assume was the effects of having the notebooks stored in a pocket or a bag while moving around under duress. A few of the words that were not clear were fairly easy to figure out. Others were much harder and I had to consult colleagues and editors to try to reach some form of consensus. By looking at the context we were on most occasions able to reach the same conclusion as far as what the intended word was. The few times we were split I chose the word that I myself felt was the most probable. If I made a mistake in trying to figure out the correct word, I take full responsibility for the mistake. However, I consider it very unlikely that any of those potential mistakes affects the overall message of the author.

Lastly, I want to make clear that my intention with publishing this text is only to convey the author's message and I hope that it will eventually reach his relatives somehow. I am not promoting or denouncing anything that he writes and neither does my publisher. The only goal is to tell his story in his own words. No one knows where he is buried or if he even received a proper burial. No relative will cry by his grave and no one had the chance to say goodbye to him. On the other hand he was able to pen his last words and if this is the only thing he leaves behind in this world I feel it is worth preserving, for the dignity that each human deserves and that perhaps someone will learn something from it.

————

I don't know you and you don't know me. And it will remain that way since my days are numbered. So why even write this diary then you might ask? That is not a bad question. I'm doing it based on hope, hope that it will reach someone that will benefit in some sort of way from what I am about to tell you. I also hope that it will reach my mother, in order for her to know my state as I move on to the next life. I have made big mistakes, some of them unspeakable and I will have to take them with me to my grave, if my enemies dignify my corpse with a burial. Only God can judge those sins. Others I will expose to the reader. Not in order for you to feel any way about it, that is outside of my control. I will only tell in order for me to share my experience and the thought process behind what turned out to be grave errors, so that hopefully whoever reads about it can learn something about how and why some people can fall into this type of trap.

This could end at any moment. I'm almost certain that I won't be able to tell my whole story. Me and two other soldiers from what used to be a platoon are on the run. As far as we know our enemies are controlling all the surrounding areas. Some of our former brothers in arms died a few days ago before our own eyes. Some of us were able to escape that same destiny, for the moment being at least. The three of us have managed to stick together and at the moment I'm writing these words we have no clue what happened to the others in our platoon that managed to save their lives a few days ago.

They might be alive still or already in the next stage of their existence, post mortem. Even though we have our cell phones we can not use them. They are all turned off. Our many different enemies that have in essence surrounded us can see any type of cellular activity. If we even turn the phones on and a signal is sent to the satellites in orbit, they can pick it up and locate us swiftly. So we are cut off from communication with the exterior world. Prayer is the only thing that we have. And at this point I am pretty sure that our prayers won't be answered. Not because He doesn't hear them, because He always does. Rather because we have done enough atrocities to put many a tyrant to shame and I believe we no longer deserve any devine succour.

Yes, we belong to that notorious group. Or in my case, I *belonged*. The group with the black banners, that misused the beautiful words on that flag for our false cause. The ones that tried to establish a self-proclaimed caliphate. We disgraced the words on the flag that we hijacked and that is right at the top of the mountain of sins that we accumulated. But my change of heart as of late is irrelevant to our enemies. They wouldn't believe me if I told them that I no longer believe in what we used to propagate. Or they might, but it won't matter as far as what they will do with me and my companions. The death sentence has been passed already. Mercy is not an option at this point. Most will say that that is just reciprocation for the attitudes that we ourselves held when dealing with our enemies and they wouldn't be wrong in saying that. I have no counter argument. That is why I have accepted this fate. But before this earthly sojourn is over I hope I get the chance to explain myself and tell the story of a fallen soul, lest you think that everyone that was involved in this whole mess was the same type of bloodthirsty psychopath.

A.

October 8th

I'm not from some ghetto in a big city in the western hemisphere. It wasn't all bad when I grew up. Both my parents worked, very hard. They did all they could for us. They are not to blame. But sometimes you are dealt cards that can't be defeated by honest living and good intentions. They migrated to America to look for a safer and better life than what "back home" had to offer. They were looking for safety and a future for their children. Soon after they made the move dad received the bad news, the type you never want to hear. "We will do our best but it might be too late. We can try chemo, we can try this and that. But we can't guarantee anything." The man fought like a lion and hung on for much longer than what was deemed possible by the doctors. God bless his soul, رحمة الله عليه. It was obviously hard when he died. The family took a hit, in many ways, including financially. My father was not what I would describe as religious. I think he had strong faith, I would never doubt that. But I always viewed my mother as the religious one. It was much more visible with her. I can't remember seeing my father pray much when I was a little kid. He didn't really take us to the mosque very often at all, except for Eid of course. But his religiosity changed the last couple of years. In the beginning of the cancer pronouncement it felt like he didn't take it very seriously, strangely enough. It was almost as if his mentality was that he was going to beat it no matter what. And for a while it seemed like maybe he would. He went blow for blow, toe to toe. But the war of attrition took its toll on him and in the last part of his life he seemed to have come to that realization. He started praying regularly. He didn't have a lot of money at all saved up but the little he had, he tried to invest in his afterlife. He put away a miniscule sum for us, the rest he gave to charity. He spent a lot of time reading the Quran. In his very last days he had to do it from his bed, my mother standing by his side next to the hospital bed with the holy book held out in front of her dying husband. I was ten years old when he passed away. It shook us, but not as much as what happened about two years before he passed. 9/11.

I still remember it well. I was eight years old at the time and was obviously already in school. After that day, everything changed. *Everything.* We found out in school. At first, I didn't really grasp it. How could I? I was eight. I remember coming home and my parents trying to explain to me what had happened. Some very bad people did something very bad. As the narrative developed in rapid fashion over the next few days, it became clear who the public was supposed to hold responsible. My parents made it very clear to me, those people who did that are *bad* Muslims. If they were even Muslims at all. And we have absolutely nothing to do with them.

My parents unfortunately, in their naivete, swallowed the popular narrative as it was spoon-fed to the masses. I didn't come to the realization of what actually happened on that notorious day and the underlying purpose until much later. It wasn't until I was close to eighteen that I started looking into the events of that day. But this is not the place for me to lay out all my thoughts on that subject. That is not what I want to convey in these pages. And others have already done a masterful job of unveiling the truth of the matter. The other thing is that you would probably call me a nut, a conspiratorial nut that is making excuses. And you would perhaps throw the rest of this text away since you would assume that I'm not reasonable. To me it is not nutty, and I'm far removed from being in a position where I can afford the luxury of worrying about what people think about my opinions. I'd rather like to think of it as not being one of those simpletons that just accepts the narrative that the mainstream media puts out there in order to dumb us down and in order to make us lazy enough to not do our own research. It's the easy way out, which I understand many prefer, it doesn't take any effort.

But all the deeper discussions about who and why are neither here nor there. Because that did not affect the practical implications that I need to tell you about. Those implications were obviously a consequence of the mainstream narrative. Soon after the event we obviously saw the invasion of Afghanistan, followed by the Iraqi invasion which we soon learned was based on a completely false pretext. What many of us did not see though, was how the conditions changed for many Muslims living in the West. Our honor and dignity became collateral damage. I refuse to believe that my father's deteriorating condition was merely a correlation to what happened after 9/11.

If you never experienced it yourself, you will never be able to know what it felt like. To go to school and all of a sudden be nicknamed "the terrorist". Ahmed the terrorist. Students screaming "BOOM" when they see you walking down the hallway. Hearing the never ending questions: Is that a bomb in your book bag? Can you call in a bomb threat so we can go home early today? Are you going to try to become a pilot after you graduate? Ad nauseum. You can't even begin to imagine what this will do to an adolescent's psyche. I went to a school where I stood out, it wasn't the most diverse student body. I only had a few other fellow Muslim students, and none of them in my class. We bonded and tried to have each other's backs. But it also inflamed the us-against-them mentality. Before 9/11 I didn't really see myself as different from the other students, at least not from what I can remember. I was so young that one would think that obviously I couldn't remember the psychological intricacies of child interaction. I can tell you one thing though, I remember it and still feel it clearly when thinking about the post-9/11 era at age eight or nine and going forward. And it didn't get better, I transferred between schools more times than I can even remember. Perhaps needless to say, I didn't finish high school. It was too much of a burden and there were other things outside of school that just felt more appealing. At least outside of school I could find some form of belonging with certain groups of friends. I didn't feel like the outcast that school assured me that I was. It was a shame, because I was good in school. It came easy to me. A lot of the stuff was boring and not stimulating at all. The classroom was not for me. But I loved English for some reason. I really liked literature. I liked reading and writing. I don't know why, I really don't know why. There must have just been something about the language that was appealing to me. I grew up in a bilingual household with Arabic as the main tongue. By an early age though, English was the language I felt most comfortable with. I even dabbled in Spanish for a short while but obviously dropped it as I dropped out of school. Alas, it was not meant to be for me in the school system and I know which incident to blame. But the things I had to suffer in school because of the 9/11 attacks was nothing compared to what I had to suffer at home.

But this is getting long-winded. I didn't mean to write this much today but I guess I needed to get my thoughts out. I don't want this to turn into some biography where I tell my life story. Nevertheless, I believe it is crucial to understand the background that produced what I became when I decided to join this disgraced group in the middle of this civil war.

My two companions are already passed out, good for them. Every minute of sleep is worth gold under these conditions. I pray that I will catch some during this night. If I'm alive tomorrow I'll continue my story, in sha Allah. ان شا الله

Ahmed

October 9th

————

Another day, another life extension. A few more breaths of air and hopefully a few more bites of something edible before we say goodbye and leave this hell on earth. It is hard to call it a countdown when one doesn't know how far away the end is. But it is inevitable, that much we are sure of. It doesn't really sadden me. I have come to terms with the fact that my life will be over before I turn twenty five. It is one of those things that make you panic when you first realize it but after you spend some time processing it you come to the realization that it is the way it has to be. And truth be told, I have seen and done things that make me not want to live any longer. The only future, in the impossible event of me coming out of this alive, would be a life of agony and mental torture. Some would say a punishment for the deeds I have done. To them I would have no counter argument to present. But that point is moot as our demise is inevitable. In the meantime I will have to fight the inner demons until the time comes. I would guess and hope a few days from now, but it could just as well be within a few hours. I'm hoping for a prolongation of whatever is left of this life only so that I can get the maximum amount of thoughts down on paper. Once I'm gone I won't be able to convey anything, obviously. So these last few moments are worth gold to me, or rather much more valuable than that mineral. Precious metals can't do a thing for me at this moment. But time can. Time gives me this soul-cleansing activity of writing and also a few more opportunities to beg Allah for forgiveness for misusing His name and His Prophet's legacy. Sins that I know I deserve never-ending torment for. Do I think that I will be forgiven? No. But I do still hope so. It's a sin to despair of the mercy of the Merciful, a sin that I was acquainted with as soon as I realized what I had done. But I slowly came to the realization that the time He has given me *after* me corrupting my soul and invoking His authority wrongfully has to have been given to me for a reason. I'm assuming it is either to get a preview of what is to come by going through the psychological torture of the mind that is a result of the things I did, and almost nothing in comparison to the punishment that awaits me. Or, it was given to me so that I might take the opportunity to repent and do at least what I can to clean my conscience to the best of my ability. Since I can not know the reason with certainty, all I can do is to try to make the best out of a dire situation and try to impose my will so that it will hopefully turn into the latter of the two possibilities.

Excuse me for losing track of my life story that I started to tell. My thoughts are moving so fast under these circumstances that it is hard to stay focused and organized in the head space. I left at the point where I was going to tell you about what was the absolutely hardest thing about the post-9/11 world that we were all forced into. The teasing in school and generally speaking all the looks and insults that were thrown my way were tough and made a big impact on me and my behaviour, and above all on my attitude. But the thing that really screwed me up was what happened to my mother. We all know how sacred the mother is for a young boy. It is the one thing that is totally off limits when it's ballbusting time. No matter what creed one holds or what the ethnicity of one's parents is, where I came from, mom was untouchable. And if someone crossed that line, it was *on*. Add to that the Muslim element of obligatory reverence for one's parents, with a major emphasis on the mother (something that Muslim parents never forget to teach their children, although they might neglect important aspects such as prayer and Quran-reading), the untouchable becomes absolutely forbidden to the highest degree. But I'll tell you one thing about my mother, she was a *proud* Muslim. Like I mentioned, my parents were not the most observant Muslims in the world. I think many other Muslims would look at our family as pretty secular. But some things were holy and never to be disrespected. The hijab being one of those things. I never saw my mother leave the house without it and I can't remember a single time when we had guests at our house and she didn't don the scarf. So imagine the horror when we walk down the street on an October day, not far from our own neighbourhood, and a man walks up and tears the hijab of my mother's precious head while yelling "fucking arab!" At first it was nothing but shock. I don't even remember the rest of the words that the wretch spewed at my mother, but I do remember that there was a torrent of insults. Me and my brother were too young to even do anything about it if we had the courage to. The perpetrator was a grown man and was flanked by at least two other men. Me and my brother were young boys who were terrified. I remember that being the first time in my life that I ever felt real *fear*. Not what you feel when your parents threaten you with punishment, not what you feel when the boys in the neighbourhood look at you funny like they have something up their sleeves. Not the sensation you get when the car hits the brakes and you realize it was a close call. Not what happens to your mind when the neighbor threatens to call the police. None of the above. This one was different. It took hold of my soul, and shook it, *hard*. The type of shaking that your organs feel. All the way up your spine. It makes you freeze and time stops. And in a paradoxical way time flies, because you stand there frozen not realizing what is going on. Nothing happens and nothing moves. The only thing you are aware of is the acute dread. And at the same time things are happening at a rapid pace all around you but you miss out on all of it. When you come to your senses it feels like you were gone for a split second, yet you understand that a lot has transpired while you were checked out. And I remember that after coming to my senses the first sensation I felt was sadness. I wanted to cry because of what I witnessed taking place, the degradation of my mother. But tears were held back by the rage that ensued. At the time I did not understand the cause of the rage. Years later I realized exactly why it appeared and displaced the sadness. It was the fact that it happened in a public space, in front of a crowd of people, and that not a single soul had the decency to say that what had transpired was wrong. No one that would stand up for the sake of justice and defend an innocent woman that had been defiled in public. It wasn't an isolated incident, that was the first of many incidents over the next few years. Some of them were even worse. Twice, *twice*, my mother got spit on by strangers. One of the times I witnessed it myself, the other she told me about. Again, I was too little to do anything about it. My older brother also saw the spitting incident. He is only three years older than me and was also incapable of acting at the time. We have a younger sister who was spared the degradation of having to watch that. If that happened *now*...you don't even want to know. I'm trying to write all this down to tell the world, or the few souls who might read it, that I'm a changed man and that I put my old self, my radical and extreme self behind me. Which I do stand by. But if anyone spit on my mother now, I would take one last soul with me to the next life.

There were also other incidents in that time period, too many to remember to be honest. Outside of verbal insults there was also hate mail, death threats and vandalising. Graffiti on our house and car for example, words I choose not to repeat in order to not inspire anyone to replicate such slander. It was unbearable, we felt like there was nowhere to run. I felt the desperation that our family was afflicted by. We tried moving, several times. It seemed like no matter where we ended up it was the same story. After a while it became paradoxical in the sense that it weakened us a lot, yet at the same time it strengthened our family. We were weak in the sense that we felt shame, we felt exposed, constantly a target waiting to be aimed at by new arrows of defamation. At the same time it seemed like our faith increased. Not really mine, at that time I don't remember thinking too much about faith at all. But it did a lot for my identity. There was no doubt any longer who I was. Before that, even though I was very young I remember struggling a little bit understanding who I was, or rather who I was supposed to be. Son, brother, mama's boy, pupil, friend… I always seemed to assume slightly different roles depending on who I was interacting with while not being truly sure of who I *really* was. After the harassments started I came to the realization of what truly defined me. I was a *Muslim*, everything else was secondary. I can't speak much for my siblings, I haven't talked to them much about how it made them feel. My mother on the other hand though was so strong. There is no person I respect more than her. The easy thing for her to do would be to hide. Stay in the house and only go out when truly necessary, and when you do go out, leave the hijab at home. Instead it seemed to strengthen her resolve. I remember seeing her pray more, read more. I don't remember her talking much about Islam to us kids outside of the regular basic stuff that I'm sure each Muslim parent tells their children. There really wasn't any preaching. She mostly just seemed worried about us and not about herself. And she worried about my father also. It was at this time that his struggle with his disease started to take a turn for the worse. It felt like until late 2001 he was landing as many punches as he was receiving in his battle with the thing that was growing inside his body. But from the moment that the incidents happened, the big ones, the hijab tearing and the spitting, he entered a losing battle with the crab. It was as if the humiliation that his family had to suffer was too much for him. Maybe not just that, probably more so the fact that he couldn't do anything to stop it. That was probably the biggest blow he had to absorb. My father was always proud and his family was the greatest source of that pride. And when the family's honour was sullied and tarnished it seemed to affect him very hard even in a physical sense, and it took away from the power that he needed to fight his illness. It was a slow deterioration that we all noticed. I remember it clearly even though it happened when I was between eight and ten. We could see his body decaying in slow motion. I remember playing with him one day at home and clinging on to him like you do when you fake wrestle with your father and I suddenly realized how thin he had become. Where there used to be flesh and at least a semblance of muscle mass there was now just bones with a skin overlay. I also noticed how thin his neck had become as I was hanging on to it. It was scary to me. It was still my father, I recognized him, but he was slowly morphing into a sad, worn down version of his old self.

I refuse to believe that my father's demise and the humiliation that my family suffered after the disaster in New York was merely correlated. To me it was and still is a fact that the former was caused by the latter. It sucked the soul out of him and his willingness to fight. He hung on for about two years but was then forced to let go. I hope and believe that he was in a good place with his Lord when he took his last breath. From the outside he looked like a broken man. At the same time though I remember him in the last part of his life reading more Quran than ever before, despite his physical limitations at the end of his sickness. He spent more time in prayer than what I can ever remember him doing before that, he was even doing it while bedridden at the very end.

It's getting late now. Both my companions seem to be in deep sleep. It's pitch black outside and a relatively quiet night. It is a great night to try to catch some sleep. I have almost given up on being able to sleep for more than forty five minutes in a row. I'm a light sleeper and with death breathing down my neck I'm extra attentive even in my subconsciousness. It is interesting that none of us react to bombs going off far away anymore. If the noise is close enough it will take your attention, but if it is in the far distance it won't even register any longer. This is when you know that you are war-damaged, when the sounds of arms and bombs get sorted out as miscellaneous meaningless noises that are not worth getting bothered by. It is as if we have lived close to a train station or a highway for a long time and it's turbulent sounds don't even bother us any longer. Except that now the things that don't register are explosions that are leaving people dead or maimed and at the same times sending countries back in time.

Abu Salih

We were able to move today, from one abandoned house to another. The scary thing is that we don't exactly know where we are moving. Is it away from the enemy or towards them? Instincts and prayers are our only guiding light in this war of darkness. My partners are steadfast, at least it seems that way. They are set to die on the ideology of this forsaken caliphate. Deep down I want to tell them that I'm no longer part of their failed desolate sect. If they are still as staunch as I believe them to be they will kill me on the spot if I open up about this. I truly want to persuade them with the few arguments I have. Most of them are emotional and experiential, not many of them logical, though a few of them are. Not that logic would be an efficient weapon in a war of ideologies with these people. It would be an honourable martyr's death, to speak the truth in front of unjust people. And I will die soon enough regardless, so why not choose the honorable path instead of the other one? My only way right now to defend that I decline being killed by my de facto comrades is that it won't give me the time to finish writing these words and cleansing my soul. That is my number one priority right now, if I succeed in telling you all that is on my mind and all that my heart contains, then I will consider coming clean in front of them. Hoping for their guidance but expecting their wrath.

Let me go back to where I left off yesterday when telling you my personal story. My father passed, while my mother continued to be a rock. She was so solid, from the outside it looked as if nothing could deter or derail her. Inside, I'm sure she went through hell. Not only did she lose her husband who had stood by her side for years and fathered her three children, but on top of that she kept on dealing with discrimination on a regular basis that she had never known before 2001. She refused to show weakness in front of her kids. My mother is by far the most honorable person I have ever seen in my life. And for her to have been disrespected and humiliated in that way must have killed her internally. But if it did, it didn't show. She was a model of patience and good character. Whatever me and my siblings lack in that department, we definitely can't blame it on her.

Our situation appeared to be inescapable. My mother saw that what was happening was affecting her children, both directly and indirectly. Directly for me and my brother who had issues to deal with in school and indirectly for our sister (and us boys of course) who had to deal with living in a fatherless home all of sudden and a mother who, though not outwardly ailing, was stressed out and had to figure out how to maintain a family and try to create some type of semblance to balance and normalcy in a world that would never be normal for us ever again. The financial strain in itself was enough to topple a family. My father was the breadwinner, he was relied on for that and assumed that responsibility gladly. My mother only worked sporadically when we were little kids. Just enough to contribute to the family's well being while putting the majority of her focus on raising her kids. As my father got diagnosed they realized that things would change. The steady stream of income which he had generated hitherto slowly started curtailing. With the welfare system being what it was and our lack of any real health insurance, my mother had to step up and work more. There was no other solution. The sicker my father became, the more she started working. And when he was gone, it was all on her. She worked three jobs to keep us afloat in this novel disastrous ocean. The one unfortunate (though while it was happening, fortunate from my and my brother's perspective) consequence was that he and I and our little sister were left alone a lot and left to our own devices. We cared for our sister and did our best, but that was not a job suited for two young boys. So when one of us was looking after her, the other one started roaming. And the streets are the streets. They have their own norms, their own rules, their own hierarchy. And an influence that can be so strong and in-fluential that a mother, no matter how loving and caring, can't compete with. Why not just move?, you might ask. We did, over and over again. With very limited financial resources it ended up being a migration from worse to worse which just added to the instability of an already volatile situation.

Mom did her best and the outside influences did their best. It was not a fair fight. My brother started getting into real trouble, and I was not far behind. School just became harder and harder to endure, new classmates almost every semester and new jokes at our expense. Clever new ways to insult us, original arab jokes and newfangled ways to insult our religion. And when mom got brought into the jokes, like it often does among boys in a playful way, our replies were not playful in the least. We got into fight after fight in school, my brother and I. As the years slowly moved along, our changing of schools was no longer due to our mother trying to relocate to find a better living situation. Rather it was a result of me and my brother getting kicked out for fighting. The only positive side effect was that I developed into a very good fighter. And I got a reputation at a young age for being a beast with my hands, I could really throw them. Now I understand that the reputation which I embraced at the time was one of the causes of my demise. The more I heard and felt that I had a rep, the more self-fulfilling it became.

My brother was always two steps ahead of me, on the path leading to self-destruction. It all but ensured that I was going to follow the same track. With no other role model to look up to, my brother became the one I emulated. He was the hero that stood up for the family's oppression and the Muslim cause. Or at least that is how I understood it as an adolescent. My mother was powerless and must have felt as such. She was forced to stay out working just to keep us alive, food and shelter came first. Pride was a thing of the past as she had to make ends meet by scrubbing floors and disinfecting toilets. Doing custodial work at a morgue on the weekends and a bunch of other types of work that many would see as demeaning and below what they accepted as decency. She had no other choice, you can't raise kids if you don't have a shelter to raise them in or food to make them grow. The adverse effect of Maslow's hierarchy was that me and my brother became raised by the streets and were unknowingly heading for a rude awakening. All mom could do was pray, and pray she did. When our paths did cross at home we often saw her on her knees with her hands outstretched in front of her, palms facing the heavens. Her prayer rug must have been of great quality to hold up. She used the same one up until the last time I saw her. It was worn out but still holding up. Yet, her prayers were not answered at the time. At least not the ones that were dedicated to me and my brother. Those for my sister on the other hand must have been acknowledged since she was saved from much of the madness that would eventually engulf my brother and I. But it was not for lack of trying on my mother's behalf. She cried tears as she prayed for us, but I guess that me and my bro had to go through what we went through for some reason that is beyond our ability to comprehend. Some of the things I do comprehend in retrospect, but much of it I don't and I have come to realize that I never will. Maybe that is for others to figure out once they read my story and attempt to solve the puzzle that is my family's life.

My hand hurts. I hope you will excuse me and allow me to continue tomorrow. I feel like my palm is cramping up. I'm not used to writing with a pen like this, and the small letters I'm writing in order to not run out of pages doesn't help either. I have been blessed with what I consider above-average handwriting so hopefully what I leave behind will be legible. It's time to put the pen down for today.

Peace

October 11th

My brother fell first and I knew I was going to face the same fate soon enough. After way too many incidents and investigations undertaken by social service workers and other authorities, they put him away at a group home, deeming the situation to be such that my mother was not fit emotionally or financially to raise three children and giving them the proper support that they needed. Why else would her oldest child rebel and break the law over and over again in his very early teens? Well, there were a bunch of reasons, many of which I already outlined for you. I guess none of those reasons were visible to the investigators and decision makers. Or perhaps it was easier to ignore the underlying causes and blame it all on this ignorant scarf wearing woman who in their eyes was incapable of providing what they assessed as being sufficient for her children. So they decided to basically remove the child from her care and place him in an institution filled with other outcasts that were just as dysfunctional as him. I know, sounds like a recipe for a disaster, right? And it turned out to be just that. He started bouncing around from group home to group home, never finding a place where he felt good. We had some access to him, but very limited. He was slipping away from us and at the same time in some enigmatic way, I felt like me and him became closer during this time. It was like we could feel each other's pain on a metaphysical level. With him gone from the household though, more responsibility fell on my shoulders. I think I must have been twelve at that time and with my mother still carrying the same load, I was left with even more obligations towards my little sister. Even though she was of course getting bigger and bigger just like us boys and could handle more of her own business slowly but surely, she still needed assistance. Or perhaps not *needed*, but my mother estimated that she did and so therefore it was the way it had to be. I believe my mother feared for her daughter. The intense trauma was still fresh in mother's mind and what she experienced as discrimination and harassment was far from over. She knew how it made her feel and she was frightened that it would happen to her beloved little girl as well. Therefore any type of protection I could provide for her was of the essence. This left me with less time on my hands to roam but the times that I did have to myself with no supervisory responsibilities and also not being supervised, I just went even more crazy than I had before. Partly because I think I had a feeling that I had to make up for lost time and partly for my brother. I knew that he lived under very strict and regulatory circumstances, though he did his best to be mutinous at every opportunity, and could not find a true outlet for his frustrations. Therefore I tried to up the ante so that his rebellion could take place vicariously through me. I had a much bigger load at home to carry and out in the streets. I had to be a revolutionary to the second degree and fight my and my brother's fight against any and everything that put us down. The authorities, the law, society as a whole, institutional racism, islamophobia, anything representing the bigger babylonian system. At twelve I felt like a one-man army fighting a multifront war against super powers that wanted to exterminate my identity and was responsible for the atrophy of my family and its integrity.

I naturally ended up with a crowd that was composed of parts that all felt marginalized just like I did, though perhaps in other ways. I used to hang out with my brother's friends when we had the opportunity to spend time outside of the household together. In my eyes it made me smarter and tougher, but now I realize that it just made me do stupid stuff earlier than what I would have otherwise. It was always a very mixed group of friends no matter where it was that we were living at the moment. A colorful mosaic of minorities whose whole would put fear in your average right leaning xenophobe. We were all minorities, outside of the occasional anglo-rebel that also had beef with society at large. What bound us together was that we felt alienated from society and at the same time oppressed and disenfranchised in different ways. Some academics would probably call this something fancy, like the alienation model. As opposed to the culturally inherent model, I guess. That's not my thing so I don't know how they label it in those circles. But I do know that there is an understanding among some so-called experts that violence, terrorism, rebellion, criminality and such is an inherent trait in some peoples that get inherited from one generation to the next. I know for a fact that that theory is bull shit. My parents were probably the two most peaceful people I ever knew. And I also know that their families in their old country are very peaceful. I remember talking one time to my friend Malik, an African American guy. We must have been about seventeen at the time. We used to have deep conversations, many times stimulated by substances as we philosophised in the neighbourhood. He was the first one that brought the idea to my attention of hereditary violence. His minority community was often accused of being violent and responsible for a lot of the very high crime statistics that the country suffered from. Many times it stretches over generations: son, father and grandfather, all well acquainted with the prison system. Which they like to use as proof for their argument that "those people" are inherently wicked and evil. Malik told me: "We are from Africa. We come from Senegal, Ghana, Ivory Coast. They have some of the lowest crime rates in the world. Four hundred years of enslavement, oppression, systematic racism, *that* is what made us this way!" I saw his point immediately, because I had felt it myself. Not like him and his ancestors, but in a different way. We had our individual struggles that were different yet overlapping. Not just me and Malik, but all the guys in our circle. There was no common cultural cause, no common religious cause. We had a variety of ethnicities in our group, as well as a variety of subcultures and religious identities. The common denominator was the socioeconomic conditions that we faced and the alienation from society, and a hindrance that we perceived from becoming productive members of society. And even if there was no hindrance, I doubt that there would be much willingness to contribute to the well being of a society that we all felt had undermined our families and targeted us for reasons that were outside of our own control.

My point here was that I firmly believe that we all ended up in that situation because of factors that we did not have any influence over. We were handed our respective conditions without having a chance to form them into something better. I'm not denying that I had volition. Today, on my way out from this mess of a world, I take full responsibility for all my actions and beg my Lord's forgiveness for my misdeeds. But I also realize that the choices that I was presented with were extremely limited and compromised by external factors. Meaning that the choices I made were not made in a vacuum, rather in extreme conditions that I, myself was not responsible for. Which opens up the door to asking the question: what type of choice is that? It is easy to judge other peoples' choices from the outside and make moral judgements about them, I know because I have been doing it my whole life. Today, I would never. There are just too many circumstances and factors playing a part in decision making (or non-decision making) that the outsider is not privy to. I now indeed believe that we, meaning me and those in similar situations, are funneled in a certain direction that will necessitate us to make destructive decisions.

This is not a petition where I beg you not to judge me. Judge me if you will and judge harshly if you want to. I am no longer in a position where peoples' opinions of me matter in any type of way. There is a much bigger judgement looming that I will face soon enough. And that Judge is just and all-knowing. So the factors that we are not aware of when looking at others' situations, He is in tune with, and He knows them better than the people involved in the situations. So I hope for mercy from Him that I cannot expect from anyone else. The thing that scares me though are the things I did while knowing I was in the wrong, the things I did at times when there was more than one way to deal with a problem and chose one of the worse alternatives. How will I be judged for the times I committed wrongs while being able to avoid it? Time will tell and in the meantime I can only hope and pray for the best and hope that Allah accepts the appeal of a soul that knows that it is over.

I wrote all that just to say that you should take those things into consideration the next time you pass judgement on a person whose circumstances you are not completely aware of. Which means *all* people. Everyone has hidden things that they never told people about, things that have happened to them and that perhaps sometimes even subconsciously affect how they make decisions. You have that and I have that. Some of the things that are truly subconscious we don't even know about ourselves, much less about others. But God *does*! And it is therefore that His judgement will reign supreme. Until that day comes, judge me as you wish but be lenient with others, because even your passing of judgements counts as deeds that you will be held responsible for and asked about in the supreme court of the hereafter.

October 12th

I need to go back in time, to when my brother was placed in foster care. I was about twelve and was heading toward the same fate as him without realizing it. For me to live without my mother was inconceivable at that age. It was a tragedy that happened to my brother but I think that I at the time saw it as a speed bump on the road that was our life, leading us to parts unknown.

I kept hanging out with some of his friends that I knew. Some of them fifteen or sixteen years old, myself being twelve at the time. I was already smoking cigarettes by eleven. Never at home, never even close to the house. My mother would have been so ashamed. Even though I knew she wouldn't, it felt like she would disown me if she found out. It would be another disgrace for the family and another thing for those who already hated us to point their fingers at. I was aware of that, but it was part of the rebellion. And the rebellion came before everything. It was the cause that was worth dying for, an attitude that I kept throughout my life and led me to join the damned group claiming to establish a caliphate. I'm getting ahead of myself, let me return to that episode later on. The way there needs to be explained first, for you to hopefully understand how I could make the decision to go all the way into the depths of destruction.

Back to the cigarettes. Like I said, at eleven I was smoking regularly. I was basically smoking before I had come to realize that my penis had more than one function. Not long after that marijuana came into the picture. The older guys were smoking hashish and weed. It didn't take me long to understand that my brother was in all likelihood smoking that stuff before he was taken away. And if it was good enough for him, it was good enough for me. Adding to the allure was the fact that it was illegal, which made it a natural part of our mission to provoke the larger social system that had as its mission to obliterate us. Of course, it cost money. That also meant that there was money to be made off of it. No great amounts whatsoever but enough to finance your own addiction while putting a few dollars (much needed dollars) into your pocket. And those extra dollars were needed at home as well. Obviously I couldn't come home and throw bills on the table, my mother would understand that something was going on. I was supposed to be in school and in need of money, not helping to provide it. So it had to be done in subtle ways, like bringing home some extra groceries. Or at times some new clothes for myself and my sister, while lying and saying that I had earned a few bucks by cleaning up at the neighbourhood corner store, or sweeping the pavement in front of the local clothing store that sells you the cheapest knockoffs imported from China. It worked for a while. The problem was that it was not sustainable since there was always the risk of getting caught which seemed to be increasing by the day. Guys got busted, one after the other. As long as they didn't catch you, the thought process was that it wouldn't happen to you.

Personally I didn't really care at that time, none of us really did. We were in the ages between twelve and fifteen and it was just modus vivendi. The way things worked where we were living. You hustle, you provide, you live with the risk and eventually it catches up to you. Live with it. I had no problem with that process, it was all I knew and it seemed natural. "They picked up 'Dulla? Too bad, hope he gets out soon and that we see him again." The thing that I always had in the back of my mind though was how my mother would react if her youngest boy got busted for selling drugs. That thought did not hold me back though, there was a greater end that needed to be reached.

I thank Allah that He protected my sister. In what is probably a natural way, my mother was always more wary of what our sister got into. She also had us as protection. Not that me and my brother were big and tough or anything, no one should have been scared of us. But we knew people that should have put fear in you, if it didn't, it was probably because you didn't know who they were. The problem with our protection was that it was more or less completely worthless if we were not around. Which my brother wasn't at first as he was bouncing around between group homes, and which I wasn't either once I got into real trouble for the time. Through what I can only believe to be divine protection, my sister never got into trouble when we were away. And to this day, alhamdulillah, she has been untouched by the madness that affected and infected my brother and I.

My first stop was a group home that was about an hour and a half away from where we lived at the time. My brother had been there previously before getting transferred to his next stop on the institutional roller coaster which is the structure that is in place for dealing with souls that are lost at an early age. The group home was in a word, chaotic. I assume that the idea behind it is to give the child structure that was deemed to be lacking in the domicile. It was the complete opposite. Any routines that were meant to be present at that place had since long ago been replaced by a culture of disorder and imbalance. All the kids seemed to be on the same wavelength when it came to provoking the people working there and the workers appeared to have created a united front to suppress the kids' revolutionary actions, at the cost of the rules that were supposedly in place and whose purpose it was to form these children into productive members of society. What happened in actuality due to the institutional decadence was the complete opposite. It created a cycle that spiraled towards a darkness that was to engulf the souls of many involved. I'm not going to philosophize in a chicken-and-egg manner about what the primary cause was. Nevertheless, what I saw was kids acting up, mostly because they felt that they should not be in this place away from friends and family that, though perhaps dysfunctional, provided meaning and security in their lives. This acting up manifested itself in various ways, all unacceptable to the workers at these institutions. The response that this triggered was often aggressive measures with emphasis on punishment, as this apparently was the only type of corrective measure that these institutions believed in. This in turn, surprise surprise, led to more rebellion which in turn necessitated stricter and harsher measures to repress it. No positive outcome was visible from my vantage point, just a spiral of destruction that was perpetually becoming more and more out of control. A destruction that left scars on all that it touched, many of those scars I believe have yet to heal. I'm not talking about mine, I feel that I have been able to process it, *now*. Which is obviously too late (unless me telling you about it in this form of a warning was the very purpose of my going through it in the first place) since I'm at my final destination in this stage of my existence. It did lead me, or perhaps expedite me towards a path of destruction. And for many of those souls that still haven't figured it out, the after effects of these group homes are still out there altering the present-day conditions of our societies in negative ways. While new herds are moved in to go through the same exercise in futility, later to be back roaming the streets with more contempt than before. Passing on their negative energy to the ones younger than them which might necessitate another herd having to be exposed to the same situation and potentially suffer from the same type of exposure and walk around with scarification throughout their youth and perchance even into adulthood. It is as if each spiral births several new spirals.

A few trips to a few of those group homes and I was on my way to the next form of institution. The juvenile detention center. I made a few visits at home. It felt like social services always had some sort of investigation going on with my mother regarding my brother and I. They seemed to realize that the group homes were not a viable solution for trying to deal with our reckless behavior. So momentarily they would let us back home until they found a group home they thought would be more suitable, the results always came back the same though. A few times, for short periods, me and my brother were home at the same time. The family was, minus dad, back together again. Those stints were short-lived though, as either me or my brother kept on getting into trouble. The times our stays at mom's house overlapped we didn't mind getting into trouble together. Our mother's situation stayed the same as before. Always working, always doing what she could to care for our sister. She did what she could for my brother and I at that time period, but I got the feeling that she, after all we had done to get in trouble, looked at us as damaged goods that did not appreciate her sacrifice. And who could blame her for that? We were indeed ingrates, there is no doubt about that. It was just that the magnetic pull of the temptations in the streets had a stronger effect on us than our mother's love, unfortunately. And pull us in they did. My brother obviously preceded me at juvy, or juvenile detention if you will. I was following close behind. But JDC was different from group homes. I can describe it in some detail in order for you to understand what it is like to be locked up in that way, and I think I will. It was another one of those situations I found myself in in my youth that laid the groundwork for what was to happen later on. Which is culminating in the situation that I presently find myself in.

But please excuse me and give me permission to tell you that part of the story tomorrow. I will get stuck here if I start thinking back on juvy, it left so many deep impressions on me and I think that I will need some time to process those thoughts before I put them down on paper.

Ahmed ibn Omar

October 13th

———

It has been so calm today. So calm that it almost worries me. Only the occasional bomb going off somewhere in the far distance, other than that we can listen to the wind blowing through the holes in the walls in this decomposing house. It is giving me a bad feeling in a way, although it is at the same time extremely relaxing to have some quietude for the first time in what feels like forever. Could it be the calm before the storm? Most likely, yes. Since calm is a forgotten concept in this region that has been plagued by nothing but turbulence and chaos the last few years. Besides that, what really worries me is that I take this silence as a sign that our opposition probably has achieved complete control of all the surrounding areas and that the signs of fighting that we hear today far away is indicating that the closest war fronts are not in our vicinity. If the enemy has truly secured a wide area that is surrounding us, it made the minimal chance that we had of survival nonexistent. It was already nonexistent to me though, so this changes nothing. But my de facto colleagues were still holding out irrational hope. And this latest development might just kill that dream. If they realize that fact I fear they will try to go out in a spectacular way. But that's on them. I still feel like I can't reason with these guys. They are too deep in the fog. Just something that suggests that I'm not part of their cause any longer could be enough for them to view me with suspicion. Which might not sound that bad to you, but let me tell you that I have seen people get killed or kidnapped based on suspicion that could never be substantiated. So for the moment I will keep on playing my role in this game. If they want to blow themselves up in order to take some enemies with them, that is on them. I'm done with the killing. My book of deeds is so heavy with sins that I just can't take it any longer. Commiting sins will take a toll on your soul. I don't care to listen to what anyone has to say that does not agree with that. You might counter with: You already have so many sins accumulated, what damage will one last sin do? Or perhaps: Will you really even feel the burden of this last sin if it is the final act that you commit in your life? To the first one I will answer: a lot! If all my transgressions were to be written out on a paper, make that papers, it would without a doubt result in a very long and ugly list. This last sin would be one of many other sins, though obviously among the very biggest ones since it would entail taking another life or perhaps even lives. But you might say that in the grand total it won't make much of a difference. I beg to differ only because of the fact that I'm completely done. I have repented to my Lord for all my mistakes that I have committed during my life and I have made up my mind and promised Him that I won't transgress ever again for as long as I breathe. Like I mentioned before, if He accepts this repentance, I don't know. I can just hope and I will keep on hoping until the very end. So what I'm trying to say is that committing that type of crime right now would not just be another sin on a long list of sins for me. Rather it would nullify my repentance and conceivably be worse than all the other sins collectively, since I would have broken my promise that I told my Creator came from the depths of my heart. I would see that as the greatest form of treachery and therefore I won't even consider doing it in my imagination. As for the second question, you would only ask it if you are ignorant of what is coming our way after our deaths or if you are a moral nihilist that does not comprehend the gravity of such an action and the consequences that it will bring to the doer. Yes, the burden one has to live with in this life would be a non-factor since this life would be over. But the soul lives on and what was a mental, spiritual and physical burden in this earthly life will transmute into a purely spiritual burden that will be more real than the type of burden we are accustomed to in this physical existence. I also believe that it will be of a higher concentration and more intense as it does not occupy several realms of one's being but rather be concentrated to one's spiritual being and that would no doubt be a more severe form of torture that is a result of a person's moral wrongdoing. With that said, I'm done with killing. I'm sick and tired of being a part of it, sick of seeing it and sick of hearing about it. If my cronies want to do that, that's on them. They are beyond being persuaded at this point, I don't think I could stop them if I tried. I hope that the next death I witness is my own. It will at least put an end to this earthly suffering, and I say that while being well aware that the suffering that could potentially await me is much greater in intensity and severity. But that seems like it can wait for a little bit, back to my story.

Juvenile detention, or juvy if you will, was way different.

Once I entered an age where I was responsible for my crimes in the eyes of the law, I was aware that juvy would most likely be my destination. My brother had told me about it through his many letters that he sent me from the inside and also during our brief phone conversations that were few and far between. He told me it was like prison, but that it wasn't really that bad. He appeared to find some type of solace there after a while. It gave him some much needed structure and routines, he told me. He found a few guys that he could hang out with and unfortunately a few that he had to watch out for. That is one of the problems with double-crossing people in the streets in the name of maintaining and providing for your family, you will make enemies along the way that might emerge at the wrong time. The one constant in his letters and calls was his emphasis on missing mom. "Please tell mom I love her and tell her I miss her so much. And kiss lil' sis." It was on the paper every time just like the date and his signature. And I could *feel* those words. When I read them, it was like they would shake my core. And when I later on ended up there myself I could understand his words at a much deeper level.

It was really smaller things that got me sent to juvy. Drug possession and some bullshit weapon charges. I say smaller things because I met people there doing time for kidnappings and murders and those types of crimes. Minors who had committed major crimes that necessitated long sentences that they began serving at juvy until they hit the age that made them eligible for the state penitentiary, where they would spend the remaining time. It was somewhat of a shock for me at first. You heard about those types of kids on the street, but you seldom met them, in my case I never did. It was almost like local legends that existed in the realm of neighborhood storytelling and whose tangible existence was more mystery than actual fact. In juvy it all of a sudden became realer than real. Those same people who were subjects of project lore were standing in the same chow line waiting for their pre-packaged lunch to be handed out. Reality hit me. The killers and robbers that I had heard about were all of a sudden right there in my midst. The prison life that I had heard about in the streets and seen glorified on TV was a reality that I was now a part of. They call it juvy, but it is semantics. It is just like a prison, just that the inmates are younger. Plastic trays with food that is just above the cut-off point for what should be considered edible. Oatmeal and something that was supposed to resemble waffles for breakfast. Lunch consisting of something like potatoes or rice with make-believe meat. The rooms were really stripped down, it was on you to make it hospitable. We had wooden desks attached to our wooden beds in one juvy facility. The other one that I ended up in later on had beds made out of metal, for those inmates that did require total isolation and were not allowed to mix with the other prisoners. They even had to go on their daily outdoor walks by themselves, poor souls. What type of human rights violation that falls under I leave for you to investigate.

The clothes were the worst, at least that is what I felt at the time. Out of all the different elements of the prison environment that made you feel like a victim, and there were many of them, the uniforms we had to wear really did it to me for some reason. It was worse than the brick buildings that constantly reminded you that you were in an institution, in case you forgot. Worse than the barbed wire resting on top of the high fences, daring someone to try to get past them. Another helpful reminder, in case you somehow forgot that your freedom did not belong to you any longer. But the clothes, that weren't even that bad if I'm trying to be objective, made me feel like an entity of sorts. It was as if the sweat pants and the polo shirts that every single one was wearing dehumanized me in some way. The terrible socks that always felt like you had worn them for a week straight, even when they were fresh out the cleaners. And the boxers that cut up your groin every time you tried to play basketball or do any other type of strenuous activity. And the most disgusting thing about them was obviously that you could not block out of your mind, at least I couldn't, how many hundreds of kids had worn that very same pair before you. Animals in their fur walked around with more dignity than us prisoners who had been beastialized behind the bars. Animals taking a peak in behind the chain link fences must have thought that the world had flipped and that *us humans* were in the zoo. And we were out in the sticks too, most of these detention centers seem to be. *Far away from civilization,* like some exotic exhibition for you to check out on a day off, if you dare approach the fence that separates you from these wild animals. The fact that the geographical isolation made it that much harder for us to receive visitors was not lost on anyone. My mother struggled to make it out there even once a week. Forget about public transportation, the whole day would be wasted just going back and forth. So my mother had to first find time in her schedule, a schedule that always remained just as busy. It had to be a day when she had no other obligations, which is close to impossible when you work seven days a week most weeks of the year. Then she had to find someone with free time and enough kindness to drive her out into the countryside in order to visit. The drive itself was close to two hours, one way. Just pulling off a visit where you can talk to your flesh and blood for a couple of hours required a lot of complicated planning for many parents and siblings. Then the time spent together was sometimes very painful, even though I have to give credit to juvy for making the visiting area pleasant. It looked much better than the rest of the prison and it was possible to get privacy for those who wanted that and there was a nice playground area for the inmates that wanted to play around with their very young siblings. The fairly good environment did little to make the conversations and meetings easier. At least it filled the function of convincing the visitors that their relative was not living in a hell hole. The big problem for me with those visits was the omnipresent thought that the unavoidable separation was approaching with each tick of the clock. It made the whole experience very bitter sweet and put a dent into what was supposed to be a joyous moment of union between loved ones. I remember having almost the same feeling the one time I visited my big brother in juvy. I think it was his first stop there, at the time I was still too young to be placed in that type of facility. I went there with my mother and I remember being happy to see my brother and feeling his strong arms embrace me as we met, and feeling them squeeze me again before departure. I remember the look he gave me as he grabbed both my shoulders with his massive palms, right before we walked out. It said: hold it down at home. With him gone it was on me. Until I got into trouble and it was all on mom again until one of us would be on the outside of an institution. Sorry, I digress. I wanted to mention that even back then I felt the anxiety of knowing that the experience of meeting someone you loved and sharing very valuable time was constantly being tarnished by the oncoming separation. It was just exponentially harder to deal with as the one being left in there. Your world changes for a few hours and you enter a make-believe realm where you are back to normal with your mother. Then that realm evaporates as her back disappeares through the exit and reality hits you like a gut punch to the solar plexus.

Often though, your situation is what you make it. And if you don't, your situation will make you. It will form you into an incarnation of the abstract reality and the environment and conditions that you are dealing with. Unfortunately for most who travelled a path like mine or a similar one, realization of this truth is only understood after the reality of the matter has left deep imprints that take a lot of time to smoothen out. So the sooner you come to terms with this fact, the better for your long-term well-being.

I will tell you something interesting about my many tours in the group homes, detention centers and prisons. At each and every stop I always had at least one Muslim by my side, and some times more than just a few. In the beginning I didn't really think about it, it just felt like a natural extension of the friend circles I had had on the outside. Those friend constellations were often very diverse, both ethnically and culturally. Culturally diverse if we looked at our parents. Obviously we all inherited their cultures to varying degrees but we also ended up having our own subculture that was formed organically in our neighbourhoods as we all brought what we had to the table. We ended up creating a smorgasboard whose national and cultural origins would be unrecognizable to an outsider due to the transmogrification of all the parts as they had formed this new whole. We had Anglo Americans, African Americans, Hispanics, Indians (including Pakis and Bangladeshis), Arabs of different kinds, islanders, you name it. Hinduism was represented, as well as Christianity of different kinds, atheism, agnosticism and of course Islam. So having Muslims in my proximity that were not family members was not a strange thing to me, it felt like they were always there for as far back as I can remember. The thing was that in the streets I saw less differentiation as far as how we understood ourselves as Muslims vis a vis the others. We were this one collective of young outcasts that were not understood by the larger system and not fully understood at home either. The only ones that could really understand us were ourselves and the religious attachment that each member of the group had did not seem to play a role in how we defined ourselves versus the outsiders.

Why this changed once we ended up in institutions, I really don't know for certain. It could have been the added layer of oppression that we perceived that perhaps made us seek out people that we could bond with extra tight for security purposes, both mental and physical. It could also have been the nature of the institutions themselves. They tend to at times, if the individual is open and ready for it, force the human being to become introspective. Introspective in the sense that they wonder about their own identity and also who they are in the grand scheme of a life that is taking the shape of a mystery. It was as if we became a group within the larger group. We still had a strong connection to the larger group of outcasts that were fighting the same battle. At the same time tough, the Muslim subgroup started building a special bond that was stronger and deeper. Don't forget that this is less than ten years after 9/11, so the anti-islamic sentiment was still very strong and could be felt (which it still can be today obviously). Not always at surface level but rather at other levels that were not perceived by the naked eye. Now when I think back on it, I really don't believe that our oppressors were always aware of what they were doing. The islamophobia that had been running rampant in the U.S. after 9/11 had been absorbed by peoples' pores in some strange metaphysical way such that the hate had become a part of their DNA and one with their being. We could see it in the looks they gave *us*, us Muslims. It was harsher and had a sharper edge than the ones aimed at our mates of other religious persuasions. The words that were hurled at us night and day which were meant to be a form of discipline, they had different acoustics when they were directed at me and my brothers. And we *all* felt it. I know it wasn't a case of me making up some scenario in my own mind in order to justify my hate towards the workers at these places. We discussed these things, me and the other Muslims. And we had all perceived the same things, in the group homes and in juvy. And later on we would in prison as well. So we knew that they were not isolated incidents or just creations of young frustrated minds. It had become institutional after infecting the workers and later on being transferred to the institutions themselves. And besides that phenomenon there were also many cases of overt hate pointed at and affecting us Muslims specifically.

I will never forget one incident. (I feel stupid writing that, of course I won't forget it with the clock ticking down like it is. All I have to do is to remember it for a few more days or weeks, at the most.) We were in juvy, at my last juvy stop before being released and subsequently passing the threshold and qualifying for an adult correctional facility instead. It was lunch time and we were all sitting at our table after having picked up our trays that had been served to us after standing in line, patiently waiting for food that none of us would even look at on the outside, no matter how hungry. Not long at all after we sat down this one brother we used to call One was like: "what the fuck?!" We all looked at him, there must have been like eight of us at that table. One, whose name was really Ridwan and was from either Ghana or Guinea (always get them mixed up), was staring at his food with this freaked out look on his face. He was like: "bro, they gave me pork!" We all leaned in to get a closer look at his tray and sure enough, the food on his plate was different than mine. So we started comparing. We were a few Muslims at the table and a few non-Muslims. The non-Muslims had all received pork that day while us Muslims had a beef dish instead. The problem was that they had made a mistake when serving One. A slip-up by the kitchen staff, I'm willing to give them the benefit of the doubt. I don't think that they would try to provoke one of us like that on purpose, they were generally the nicest people working there. But One was freaking out and understandably so. The one thing that our parents pound into our minds as soon as we are able to understand them is that swine is not for us. For many of us growing up in Muslim families the swine prohibition is way more emphasized than, lets say, the prohibition against alcohol or fornication. Probably because it's the one thing that we can understand and also come in contact with at a very young age, as opposed to intoxicants and the temptations of the opposite sex. So it really gets ingrained into our very beings and a disgust develops towards that nasty animal. All the Muslims I grew up with, no matter how secularized, would never even look at a hot dog even though their ribs were showing from hunger. So One's reaction was understandable. He raised his voice to the point where one of the COs nearby started approaching the table just to see what the fuss was about. This CO in particular was not our favorite, none of the guys liked him. It felt like he always brought an attitude to work, the type that seemed to think that the little bit of authority that his uniform gave him also made him a superior human being compared to us. He would constantly give off these disrespectful remarks that were not offensive enough to get upset about, yet insensitive enough that one would not forget it easily. When he came near the table he already had that smirk on his face as he was ready to get smart with us. He approached until he was within arms reach of One and looked at him with a countenance that asked: what's the matter, without having to utter the question. One looked up at him and exclaimed blaringly with a voice full of agitation: "they gave me pork! I don't eat this shit."

A few of us chuckled, not because the mishap was funny in any type of way, but rather because of One's cadence and mannerism. The unexpected reply came so fast that it must have been premeditated: "Yeah? What do you want me to bring you? A banana? Isn't that what you Muslim monkeys eat?" Before anyone at the table could even react to the insult, One's food tray violently made contact with the CO's eyebrow and the grown man started falling towards the ground. Before he reached the floor One was already swinging his fists at him in full force. None of us even had the chance to act, we were frozen as we witnessed this explosion of fury unleashed from the depths of our companion's being. Just as we instinctively rose to our feed, four COs rushed One and pinned him to ground while locking both his arms behind his back. Batons were pulled and driven into One's neutralized body. His screams were not those of pain but rather insults with the foul mouthed CO as its target. Blood had already started to flow from the man's brow as he stood up. We all sat down as the officers that were constraining our brave companion threatened us with the same treatment if we remained standing. They removed One from the commissary while he was putting up a brave fight, though limited by the cuffs they had fettered his wrists with behind his back. The injured CO was swiftly helped out of the dining hall while we sat there looking at each other with a combination of shock and awe in our gazes. The result of the ordeal ended up being five stitches on the CO's eye brow and a stint in solitary confinement for our brother Ridwan. I assume that he also received a nice write-up in his journal that would make life much harder for him the day that he would be transferred to an adult correctional facility. How long he had to be in the "hole" I never got to find out since I was released roughly a week later. I left juvy for the very last time. The next charge that stuck would send me to the major league, I was done with the minors. And I was also running out of strikes and getting sick and tired of the institutional environment, yet in some absurd contradictory way I was getting comfortable in the system. As is the case for many who become institutionalized early in life and fall into the negative spiral that consists of stint after stint at various correctional facilities. From an outside perspective this might seem extremely odd. Don't forget though that many people that end up in this predicament come from households that are extremely broken down and fragile. Abuse and addiction seem to be regular parts of everyday life for many families whose children end up institutionalized early on. That wasn't the case for me, as I have already told you. I had a completely different set of circumstances that happened to derail me. I'm speaking in a general sense, based on the many stories that I have heard from countless inmates. So when you end up in a place, or places, that have food that is good enough not to discard it, friends that might actually happen to understand where you are coming from, as well as a much needed structure in the form of routines, for many it is a form of normalcy that is welcomed. Also a normalcy that many end up returning to when the apparent freedom in the outside world gives them more of a burden than actual enjoyment. Parole officers to meet, piss test to take, bills to pay, responsibilities to honour. For many the stability of the institution and the extended family of like-minded fellows present a more appealing alternative than the one that society hands you.

For me it was not a case of finding a lot of comfort in the facilities, I loved my mother and our home. It was more so the extremely hard magnetic pull from the streets that made me end up in the same type of trouble with the law, over and over again. After a few bits I started developing a love and hate relationship with juvy and its successor. I hated the physical place, the walls, the halls, the food, the stainless toilets and sinks and COs. But I loved my fellow brothers who were in there, the fellowship, the brotherhood, the bond. You couldn't put a dollar value on a brother like Ridwan. He was the first person among my peers that showed what loving and honouring your religion and your self worth meant. In retrospect, was it correct what he did when he smashed that CO's eyebrow in? Today I would say no, it was an overreaction and the consequences he had to suffer were not in proportion to the insult. If I could ask One about this today I'm sure he would still stand by his actions (lol). A better and more fitting reaction would have been to use that sausage eating cannibalistic pig's wittiness against him and return the insult with even more flair. But at *that* time, it was what all needed to witness. One basically showed us that there are two things you will never be able to joke about with me, my religion and my skin color. It was as if he took one for the whole Muslim team while giving us collective strength at the same time. He set the example. Like I said, I left that place not long after that whole ordeal went down, but I'm pretty sure that no CO tested his luck by provoking any of the Muslim inmates after that.

Needless to say, Ridwan was a major inspiration for me. But he wasn't the last and he wasn't the biggest. I would meet two people that *really* changed my life when I made my one and only stop at the adult correctional facilities. I believe I first set my foot there about a year after being released from juvy for the last time. I will have to save this story for tomorrow's writing session, assuming there is one. In sha Allah! I have to say that it is the most crucial part of my life story if I try to analyze what exactly led to the present plight that I'm in, and I feel that I should take some time and try to recall as much of the details as possible before I put pen to paper and try to lay it out to you. If I make a mistake when writing this there is no form of editing tool that I can use to go back and change things. I can tear pages out of this notebook and rewrite them of course, but that is not a viable option as time is running out. So I will proceed with caution in order to not give you a version of my story that is not fully in line with what I experienced. With that said, I will sleep on it and collect my thoughts and search my memory for the details of what was the source of the biggest transformation that I went through in my life.

October 14th

It's getting late now. We just prayed the sunset prayer, me and these two guys. I will write from now until the time for the night prayer arrives. Then I will continue until these eyelids start weighing so much that my eagerness to write won't be able to keep them from falling completely and taking my soul into the absurd and scary dream world that awaits me every time I leave my waking state.

Something pretty hilarious happened today, one of the few instances of laughter that I could share with my companions. Laughter that is truly needed in order to maintain some form of sanity in this preposterous reality that we are stuck in right now. I will leave that story for tomorrow though, if the morrow arrives. It's funny enough to tell, but not important enough that I can give it precedence over my own story.

I have thought a lot about what I promised to ponder when I left you last night and want to put all those thoughts down on paper before they become fleeting. So I will pick it up where I left off last night and see how long I can go before sleep overpowers me or my right hand starts begging for mercy.

So I left juvy for the very last time feeling confident that I would never see it again. Not because I had made up my mind to stay away from activities that could lead to being arrested, but rather because I had a birthday coming up that would put me over the age limit of people that were eligible for being detained as juveniles. I was fully aware that if I was to be arrested one more time I would be tried as an adult and treated as such by the law. It had already happened to my brother who was serving a sentence of about six months when I came out of juvy. He was due to come home around two or three months after I came home and I remember really looking forward to being with him for the first time in what felt like forever.

When I became free I went right back to my mother's house. I wanted to make up for lost time even though I know that there is no way to make up time to a mother who has been deprived of many months together with her children. However, I felt an obligation to do my best and be there and support the family in the capacity I was able to, it was the least I could do. My mother (I'm tearing up as I write this) accepted me with open arms, although I knew deep inside that I did not deserve that type of welcome. She had taken care of our little sister (who all of a sudden didn't appear that little any more) all by herself while me and my brother had been away, only returning home for short stints before once again being hauled off to some form of imprisonment. What I'm most ashamed of right now when I think back on it is that I could not be determined enough at that point to say that enough is enough, I need to stay home and out of trouble for the sake of my mother and sister. I was close to legally becoming an adult, yet the responsibilities of adulthood was something that was very distant from my ambitions. Sure, I was at home and tried my best to help out, but at the same time I was waiting for my brother to join me so that we could keep on doing our thing in the streets.

I started hustling pretty much as soon as I came back home. At the same time I held down a legit job at a local grocery store. It was mostly to save face in front of my mother. I didn't work many hours a week at the grocery store, but enough to explain where the money I used to pay all the bills came from. Most of my income was of the non-taxable variety, straight from the streets. So my legit job was my side hustle (the irony). Overall, it was a good time in my life. I was able to spend quality time with my mother and sister. My sister started being out of the house more, she always used to be such a shy homebody, but she was getting deeper into her teens and new things started to become attractive and interesting to her. Thank God, alhamdulillah, she always kept good company and to this day I never saw her get in trouble. Not because of anything I did, all the credit goes to our mother. My presence just added to the miraculous nature of her being able to be saved from all the corrupting elements of society that me and my brother fell prey to.

I remember that this period of freedom was the first one where I really started to think more about my religion. Islam was on my mind more often than not, undeniably inspired by One's heroics in juvy. That incident strengthened my identity in some strange way. I started to feel prouder in some odd way about being Muslim and the fact that my sister started walking around with the hijab meant the world to me. She seemed to be taking after my mother, alhamdulillah. Mother's strong character and determination seemed to have been inherited. They both walked around with pride while being weighed down by the tragedy of having the household's leader fall prey to disease and also burdened by two sons/brothers that were living lives which were morally unacceptable and spending more time behind bars than in society. When I saw my sister like that it made me so proud, so honoured. I had almost come to take my mother's honor for granted since it had been a mainstay throughout my life, while as an older brother I was constantly worried about my sister due to brotherly love and a sense of responsibility to protect her with no father around. At that time, if anyone would even have looked at my sister the wrong way… I wouldn't even need a lawyer for that one, just accept the sentence, do my time and keep my head high and feel dignified that I defended my sister's integrity. Fortunately, it never came to that. That's just how I felt at the time though, it was as if Islam was anchoring its roots in my heart in a way that made me attached to what had always been apart of my life, just that at that point the relationship with my deen, with my religion, was becoming much deeper. I had some talks with my mother where I brought up the topic of our faith. She seemed to be positively surprised. She was, and still is the type of woman that is all action and not a lot of talk. For her, religion was very sacred, but also something that was rather private. She was not big on encouraging us to go to the mosque or really show our religiosity in public in any type of way. The hijab she wore meticulously was the only real sign of outward religiosity. Obviously that was enough to trigger attacks from all types of islamophobes and racists, but I think that an objective observer that just looked at her daily routines and how she lived her life in the public sphere wouldn't necessarily come to the conclusion that she was a devout person. At the same time she was the best exemplar of pristine morality I have ever seen. Our discussions about Islam and the opportunity to pick her brain a little bit on some of the basic questions I had, strengthen my faith some more, without a doubt.

My brother finally came back, which we were both extremely happy about. My mother and sister too, obviously. It was the first time that the entire family had been together in a very long time. I have to think that it was extra special for me and my brother though. We always had a strong bond, a bond that had been strengthened by us going through similar experiences in the streets and also in the various institutions that we came to frequent. During the times that we were both away, which felt like a rather large majority of the time, our communication consisted of letters and greetings coming from our mother and sister when they happened to visit us. Those letters were worth more than gold to us while we were imprisoned. I'll tell you, when you are locked up and you get that envelope handed to you with handwriting that you recognize… there is no better feeling behind bars. At least there wasn't for me.

I liked to read before I started getting locked up and the solitude that I faced in there took my reading to new levels. My brother also found his love for books after getting locked up and we both used our increasing reading skills to express ourselves in writing to each other. Some of these letters would go on for pages. It wasn't always the deepest content. Some of it was reminiscing on the past, writing about our family and a lot of it was just an update of what was happening in the monotone environment of the institution that we happened to be in at that moment. Still, just hearing my brother's voice through the handwritten words on those wide-ruled papers enabled me to feel his presence, and that was big for me. He was the closest person to me and the one who could understand me the best. So while we were physically separated we could still feel each other's heartbeats through the ink.

We hung out a lot when he came back home, both of us hustling and helping out at home, supporting mom and keeping an eye on lil' sis. Religion became a topic of conversation that would appear more and more frequently, both between my brother and I and in our group of friends. It was still at a very rudimentary level, not advanced at all. Any nine-year-old Pakistani from Islamabad would most likely put us to shame. Nevertheless, slowly but surely our faith that we had inherited from our parents started meaning more in small increments as time moved on. It still did not affect our daily lives much at all if you saw how we lived from an outside viewpoint. Nothing in our lifestyles would make you think that we were religious in any traditional sense, but internally, at least I started to feel "more Muslim". Unfortunately that feeling was not strong enough to influence our moral compasses. My brother would mention going legit from time to time, leaving the hustling and the criminal lifestyle whose end result we had both seen several times up close. When he mentioned it though, it sounded more like some distant fantasy than a reality that was within reach. It was a possibility, no doubt about that, even though there were a bunch of obstacles. The first one being a rap sheet that was much longer than our list of degrees and work experience. The second one was having first and last names that would make Homeland Security lick their lips and start salivating. Those factors added intensity to our already existing victim mentality. If I'm being completely honest, it was a very convenient excuse to just keep on making money the illegal way and perpetuate the downward spiral we had been travelling on for so long. I think we both used it in order to try to rationalize our behaviour and justify not striving for any type of reform in our personal lives. It led to us living double lives in a way, one out in the streets where we had images to maintain in order to solidify our standings amongst our peers and another at home where we tried to be upstanding sons and brothers to a woman and a young lady who we knew were in need of our presence and support. I look back at this time that we had together, me and my brother, as a very crucial time in my life. It was not during that period that any major change happened to me, but rather it was a timespan full of potential where I could have taken my life in a different direction if I had really made my mind up. Which i did not. It was a struggle with my consciousness and I imagine the same held true for my brother. I can only speak for myself of course, though I feel fairly certain that my brother was going through a very similar phase around the same time. He had just gotten out of jail and it sounded a lot like he had no intentions of going back there. At the same time, our sense of religiosity was on a steady incline, which should have given us motivation to stop doing some of the things we were engaged in to make money and to be frank, some of the things we did just because we enjoyed them. Now I understand that what I was dealing with at the time was a serious case of cognitive dissonance. My soul was telling me to get my life on the right track, stop engaging in crimes and all types of activities which I knew were haram. At the same time I was forcing my body to partake in the same old activities which had only brought hardship upon myself and the people closest to me. It is hard for me to know what to make of that form of religiosity that I was feeling at that time. On the one hand, it didn't steer me in a morally positive direction. I kept on living my life more or less like before. One wouldn't be wrong to say that it didn't have any effect on my daily activities and the manner in which I lived my life. On the other hand, it made me *feel* something I had never felt before. I perceived God's presence in a way I had never before. I felt aware of Him all the time, He saw my actions, He heard my words. It didn't stop me from commiting sins, but it did weigh my conscience down in a way that up to that point I had never experienced. I *felt* more religious, Islam started meaning something to me in a way that it hadn't prior. To be honest, before that specific time period I viewed Islam, I viewed being a Muslim, as something that I and my siblings had inherited from our parents. It was another demographic box to check. Just like we had an ethnicity, a language, a physical appearance… we also had a religion. Of course we had, ipso facto, since our parents did. It was one of the many things that got passed on to us. I was prideful of it before, very much like I was prideful of other family traits and cultural elements that we held dear. It was a bigger part of my identity than the other things that our parents gave us, but I think that was more so a result of our religious affiliation being the main target for all the hate we received. The fact that it was attacked blatantly made it something that became extra important to me and a part of my identity that I became extra fond and protective of. Still, it lacked meaning. I had never sat down and pondered: what does it *mean* to be a Muslim? It was during this time period that I asked myself that question for the first time. I did not find a clear answer.

One of the problems was that I didn't find anyone that could provide me with an answer. My mother did her best to satisfy my inquiries and I appreciated her efforts. Unfortunately I had a very hard time relating to her answers and I couldn't understand how they were supposed to help *me* in *my* situation. I don't blame her at all for not having the tools to adapt her discourse to mine, she didn't grow up on these streets and in these institutions. On the flip side, the people I knew that had gone through what I had gone through and were going through the same type of struggle, had the same types of questions as I did and the same lack of answers. This included my brother and all my Muslim friends. We were left to navigate the ever confusing terrain that we found ourselves in as young adults in America, without a compass or a map.

Many paths laid before us and the choices were ample, most of them leading down the road to destruction. We were on a treasure hunt with blindfolds on, only having each other to lean on for support and advice. The blind leading the blind towards the unknown.

The next big thing that happened was that my brother got busted, again. He had already done a short bit at the adult facility before rejoining the family this last time. So he knew more or less what to expect even though they were to send him to a new facility. The big difference was that this was a four-year term with a possibility of shaving off a few months for good behaviour, which was far from a lock. This meant that he would be in his mid-twenties when he got out, with most of his youth spent behind bars. Talking to him over the phone, he didn't sound too distressed. He was down but not out. He knew he messed up by hanging out with a certain crowd and messed up even more by carrying a piece, an automatic sentence that his lawyer would not be able to avoid even with the best finagling. He sounded like he was ready to take full responsibility. Previously both me and my brother always tried our best to rationalize our criminal endeavours by pointing at our situation and the forces at play that were hellbent on making our life a living hell. And those forces were still there and are still there today for certain. This time around though, my brother never mentioned them when we talked, which we both had always done previously as soon as we ended up in trouble. It was always so much easier to blame the other for one's mishaps. For some reason his tune changed and he sounded more introspective during the few times we talked as he was in pre-trial detention.

Little did I know that the day before he got busted was the last time that I would ever see him and that those brief conversations over the phone would be the last words spoken between us that were audible. Had I known, I would have appraised all of those moments in a different way. Instead this text that I leave behind will be my goodbye. My beloved brother! I wish we could have embraced while knowing that we were saying farewell to each other. Or at least that we could have had a heart-to-heart over the phone one last time. Alas, it was not meant to be. Allah wrote that this would be our destinies and I will accept it faithfully, sad at its reality, yet content with the plans of the Planner. I remember what you wrote to me those last few times via mail. I used to treasure your letters in prison. I scoffed at what you told me in those last two letters and I'm assuming that you could sense that in the tone of my replies. It was the mindstate I was in at the time. It's extremely difficult to explain, even though I will give it a try in what remains to be written in this memoir. I was so close-minded at that particular time that anything that clashed with the worldview I held then, I automatically discarded as absurd. I want you to know that I won't be dying in that frame of mind. I left it behind me and I have changed my attitude regarding a lot of things as they relate to our religion and our place in this world. This change won't undo any of the disastrous things that I have been the cause of, but I do hope that it will count for something with our Lord. In addition to that, I want you to know that I'm not the same person that rebuked the positive messages you sent me at a time when I was not able to receive them and comprehend them. You were on a path and I sincerely hope that you are still on it and find strength in it. I hope, in sha Allah, that God has great things in store for you. I can sense it. My fate is sealed, while your book is still being written, so make it a happy ending and not a tragedy like mine. I know I don't have to tell you the following, but I will anyway. Take care of mom and lil' sis. Because of my mistakes you will have to carry twice the burden, which I know you are more than capable of. You were always the strongest one of us. You will deny this because of your new-found humility, but deep inside you know it's true, I was always weaker. It's not arrogance on your behalf if you recognize your superiority over me, rather a source of increased reward if you recognize it as a gift from Allah to be thankful for. I don't know which of these pages will survive, if any, and I don't know who it will reach. If you are the recipient, hug and kiss mom from me and tell her I love her and always did. I was terrible at verbalizing it, I hope she could *feel* my love during our times together. The fact that I did not tell her how I felt to her face eats at me to this day. I should have been expressing it to her over and over again. I'm sure she knew, but I imagine that there can't be many moments of joy on this earth greater than a parent hearing the words "I love you" from their child. I'm truly sorry, to all of you. Try to let my care and love towards both mom and our sister live on vicariously through you. السلام عليكم و رحمة الله

Ibn Husayn

———————

I promised to tell the story from yesterday. I'm tempted to just pick up where I left off yesterday since I feel like I'm in a good flow with my writing and many details have come to my recollection as I have been writing and thinking these last couple of days. But a promise is a promise and it should be kept.

So yesterday morning we were sitting in this abandoned house and coming to the collective realization that we are very close to running out of food. We still have some money, but unfortunately it is not edible. We all understood that we have to go and buy food for our survival. The obvious problems were: where are we going to buy it and who will take the risk of going. We still had a fairly good awareness of our surroundings and we knew that a smaller town exists south of us. By car, probably not more than ten or fifteen minutes. One would need something 4-wheel driven though, as the terrain basically consists of sand and rocks and is rather bumpy. We estimated (correctly it turned out) that walking that distance would take roughly an hour, more or less. The last intel we had on the town was that it was rather calm. It was a town that was under our control a few months back but then we lost it to the opposition… one of the many oppositions. Like many other towns that we had once conquered and then lost, the locals seemed to rejoice at our loss of control of their hometown. No matter who came to "liberate" them they seemed to prefer them over what they deemed to be our tyrannical rule.

The irony being that we labeled ourselves as liberators when we were conquering town after town in all the directions of the compass. Specifically we claimed to liberate them from the oppression of the Syrian government, but also from their traditions that had veered far away from Islam into an unrecognizable version of the religion that moreso resembled paganism than the pure teachings of Islam. Anyhow, they were happy to see us go and alert to the danger of us coming back. We had been labeled a major enemy to the civilian population, on the same level as the government's oppressive forces. Which meant that if one of us was to be detected while going into town for food, alarms would sound and it would mean the end for the person detected, barring an unlikely escape.

The big question obviously became: who is going to go? We tried to settle it in a few different ways. At first I thought we might default to who was the hungriest, but I realized that we were all already on the brink of starvation. We batted around basing it on seniority, the youngest would go. The problem was that the youngest had spent the most time in the caliphate and could himself argue that he was senior to all of us. We also thought about basing it on the amount of battle experience, we soon realized that it would be idiotic to send the person with the least experience if he had to fight his way out. We had to settle for an old classic game of rock-paper-scissors. I saved myself in the first round, I threw rock while both of them threw scissors. I became a spectator, feeling relieved that I was not the one that had to risk my life during a grocery run and at the same time terrified that my next meal was dependent on a guy with a death sentence on him. They threw and tied three times in a row. Rock versus rock. Paper versus paper. Rock versus rock again. Finally the tie was broken as one threw scissors and the other paper. Curse words filled the room from the esophagus of the loser. This was followed by reminders from the winner that the loser should beg God's forgiveness for the profanity filled outburst. This loss and the loser's upcoming mission was part of God's decree that we shouldn't question, rather we should accept it in humble submission. Which we all did, for two of us it was easier than for the third. At this point, hilarity ensued.

He obviously couldn't head into the settlement the way he was looking. Any outward appearance that gave away his affiliation would have been equal to a death sentence. His garb alone would be enough, so that had to be addressed first and foremost. In addition to that, his long beard was a dead giveaway. The long, wide and at times unkempt beard had become a trademark. Unfortunately, for all those honest law-abiding Muslims who honored the tradition of adorning themselves with a pronounced beard on their chins, which had for many become associated de facto with the scums in our sect. Changing his clothes was not the biggest deal, we all had an extra set of basic clothing necessities in our backpacks. He could just go in a plain t-shirt and his baggy pants, but that would just look… weird. We ransacked the house we were in and found a decent pair of jeans and a green polo shirt, not far from the style of the locals in the area, so it had to suffice. The beard… well, it just had to go. Much to his chagrin. I and the other companion told him that he had to do it. God wouldn't see it as a sin for him to trim his facial hair if he did it for the greater good, the greater good being basic foodstuffs for our survival. Hesitating, and with a bad mood, he walked upstairs for his makeover.

About twenty minutes later he walked down with the most pathetic look on his countenance as we stood there anticipating his fashion statement. At first sight both of us doubled at the waist from laughter and after a short while our legs could not support our howling torsos. The guy came down looking like a recovering heroin addict. The jeans were at least three sizes too big in the waistline and were supported by a tightly girded belt. The green polo looked ridiculous on him and his face looked like Edward Scissorhands had groomed him with a blindfold on. The guy had cut his beard with his razor sharp combat knife. It must have been such that once he realized that he couldn't manage to give himself an even trim, he tried to shave it all off nice and tight, and after afflicting his own face with several cuts he must have understood that the instrument in his hand was not suited for facial hair grooming. The man had cuts on both his cheeks and his neck. With fresh blood exiting the wounds in tiny streams. Straight up crack addict coming out of the alley. We couldn't control our laughter while this poor bum was so ashamed of his transformation that he couldn't partake in our outburst. He started cussing us out again, using diction that I don't have the decency to repeat. So swiftly had he forgotten our earlier adminishions of keeping God's decree in mind and submitting to it in humility. He set out with a couple of plastic bags in his pockets that he could use to carry the groceries back with. The military backpack would have been another giveaway. Imagine if he got caught because of the backpack and what ended up looking like a botched surgery on his face was all for naught.

Then the fun was over and the wait started. This was unlike any other wait I had ever endured previously in my life. In war, you wait a lot. Half of war is patience, as you are constantly waiting on intel to reach you that will determine your next move. Act in haste and it might be your very last act. This wait was of a different kind though. After the stomach cramps from the laughter went away, we both turned to prayer when we realized that our fate was to be determined by a guy looking like a dope fiend that went on a mission in order to extend our lives. It was three plus hours of excruciating suspension. We understood early on that if he was not back after about four hours, he probably wasn't coming back. After five, we might as well do the funeral prayer in absentia. And after that try to figure out what to do about food. I tell you what, not in order to gross you out, but rather in order to give you some insight into the human psyche. When you get hungry to the point that you feel like your ribs are about to poke through your skin and you have no clue if you will ever see another meal, that is when you for the first time in your life *really* start considering if you would eat human flesh in order to extend your lifespan or if you would rather wither away in excruciating agony. Full disclosure, I came to the conclusion that I would rather starve to death slowly. But the option will be considered at one point when you are staring starvation straight in the eye.

Fortunately for all of us he did return, both exhausted and elated. He seemed to want to tell us all about his adventure. All his words fell on deaf ears as we started looking through his bags to see what we would be eating for the next few days. Flat bread, canned lentils and chickpeas, dried fruit and nuts and a few random items. Good choices, all high in calories and able to last long in the dry heat. As far as beverages go, we don't have anything except for tap water which I am convinced will give me an ulcer any day now, and some cheap tea bags that we found in one of the cupboards. We had a simple meal of bread with salted chickpeas, careful not to overeat in order to make it last for as long as possible. It will sound ridiculous to you, but it was a *great* meal. I'm not going to say best ever, because I know that objectively speaking I have had better meals in my life. The circumstances can not be neglected though. The fact that you were just uncertain that you would ever see another meal, in combination with extreme hunger *and* also not knowing if this will be your last meal, adds more flavor to a dish than your favorite chef would be capable of.

I want to get back to my personal story. That was a long detour, though I perceived it to be necessary. Not for my overall story, it was in the larger scheme a completely meaningless event without a deeper meaning. At least it gave you a short glimpse into my daily life here and also, and more importantly for me, it gave me a much needed outlet to relive a good laugh. Writing is at this moment hindering me from crossing the threshold which separates sanity from insanity, so that story was therapeutic and also made me giggle while thinking back on the incident. Laughter is a much needed commodity for me right now that is immensely scarce.

Back to where I stopped narrating yesterday. My brother got locked up and we would never see each other again. We didn't know this at the time of course. He got a rather long sentence. His history of criminal activity and his previous sentences didn't do him any favors. He would be gone for a while at a high security prison and we figured that we would be in our mid twenties the next time we laid eyes on each other outside the prison walls. Our mother was crushed. She had become used to me and my older brother getting into trouble and going away to different places for varying amounts of time. It had become a dependable pattern that didn't break, year in and year out. Still, her motherly love forced her to hope that the last time was the *last* time. And when it wasn't and it also turned out to be the longest sentence to date, it hurt her more than the previous ones. As for myself, I went back to my old routine when I was the only male in the household. I tried to be home a little bit more, help mom with any necessities around the house and any contacts with hospitals, authorities and such. My sister was a big help when it came to those things this time around. She was about to finish high school and was coming into her own as a young woman. I tried to dedicate as much time as I could to be there for her in any type of way. She needed security and a male to lean on and if it wasn't me, it could become the wrong male. It wasn't like I was over-protective or anything like that. I just made it clear that I was available, and that if she needed anything, that she should come to *me*.

It turned out to be perhaps the steadiest period of my life. I really scaled back on illegal activities and held down a couple of honest jobs for a long while. I had one at a grocery store close to home and another in a department store in a mall, this one further away, but close enough that the bus was not a bad option. I was making some honest money, most of it went to the household. I was able to put a little away with each paycheck that came, it was the first time in my life that the money I received did not all at once evaporate like ethanol. From my side activities, if we can call them that, I still had a small but steady income. But my hands weren't really that dirty because of it. Having been around for so long in the neighborhood, I had reached the point that I didn't have to do a lot of the daily activities that usually come with making money on the streets. There were still some risks here and there, but I avoided the daily chores. This was partly due to my seniority and partly me just being my older brother's little brother. He had pulled a heavy load for our little organization for years and was now away as a result of his involvement. His pedigree had to be respected and me being related to him by blood made me elevate in the ranks automatically, those were the statutes. I didn't care that much for it though, my heart was not really in it any longer. It felt like it had run its course. The results were not exactly enviable. A few did really seem to make it and lived a good life as a result of hustling, but they were a very small minority. Most suffered the same fate as my brother just had, and my brother's sentence was relatively mild compared to what others around us, especially the generation before us, had to suffer. The problem is that you might be ready to leave your past behind you and move forward, whilst your past is not yet ready for you to move on. It's one thing to have the will to change, it's another to take all necessary measures to enact said change. I thought I was doing what was right, which I was to a certain extent. I was there for my mother and sister more than I ever had before. I held down a couple of honest, steady jobs (I was actually paying taxes! LOL, still can't believe *that* happened). I didn't mind working, it could get monotonous but the boring monotony was outweighed by constantly seeing many new faces every day. How much they enjoyed seeing my face, I don't know. Several customers apparently complained to my supervisors that I was staring at them in a menacing way. Where I come from, we just called that having your eyes open. My bosses explained to them that it was not my intent to be menacing and that I was actually a really nice guy. They were nice to me, they had no real obligation to keep me employed, they could have just replaced me with whoever that didn't look deranged when gazing at the customers and they would have saved themselves some trouble with the very people that kept their businesses going. The stare was something that I developed in juvy. It was a totally subconscious acquisition. That type of gaze was a form of survival instinct that evolved in that type of environment in order to not become prey in the jungle that those institutions are. If we lock eyes, rest assured that I won't be the one to look away. That habit doesn't go away just because one walks out of the institution and into society. I still have it as a matter of fact, but I don't believe it is as pronounced as before. Thanks to God's grace and my bosses' generosity, it didn't hinder me from working. Soon enough, something else would.

Everything was moving along rather smoothly, just as I described earlier. I had a decent amount of honest work. Things were well between me and my mother and sister. The void left by my brother was still very noticable. It wasn't new, him being away had become standard for our family. The difference was that this time we knew that we would not be seeing him for a few years. I still put in a minimum amount of work for our little team in the neighbourhood. I wasn't serious about it at all, I felt like a placeholder for my brother. He had done a lot to become "somebody" in our hood, so I thought his presence should still exist vicariously through me. On top of that, all the guys who were still really engaged in that life were my friends. "Friends", is a relative term I have come to learn. At the time that is what I called them though and viewed them as such. In hindsight, only a couple of guys out of that rather large group would I consider to be people I would ever trust. Back then, I didn't know better and hanging out was still a part of my lifestyle that I not only didn't see as negative but it was also a regular custom that was basically second nature to all of us.

Then one evening, it came crashing down. It was a regular type of hang out, there were about eight of us in this one apartment. We just called it "the spot". Guys playing video games, guys talking shit. A few were smoking, a few were drinking. Me and this guy I had spent some time with in juvy were playing chess on that particular night. The police knocked and yelled at the door. Most of us froze as is natural when the police are about to confront you, a couple of the guys started scrambling. I wasn't worried at all. In my mind, all the police would find was some underaged kids drinking a little bit and smoking some weed. It probably wouldn't even be worth doing the paperwork for those guys. Usually when that happens they will dispose of the drugs and pour out the liquor, then give you a lecture about how bad it will be next time they catch you, followed by bla bla bla. In one ear, out the other. Not this time, they came in with what looked like the SWAT team. Weapons drawn, pushing everybody to the ground. They basically disabled us and then started turning everything upside down in the apartment. My first thought as I layed there smelling the old carpet was that they were just wasting their time.

My second that was: F@%#, someone has broken the rule. We had one major rule in our group, do whatever you want on the side, but DON'T BRING WORK TO THE SPOT, EVER. I hadn't been lying there sniffing the old persian replica for more than a minute before one of the cops (or whatever they were) yelled: bingo! They found something. And they kept on finding things. Some smartass (or asses, still don't know) had brought drugs that he (they) was selling, pretty large amounts and different varieties. They took us straight to the station and locked us up. I knew the procedure, nothing new. I thought I would just wait it out, the responsible one would admit to it so that the rest of us could go on with our lives. I was wrong about that. There were a few of the guys there that I suspected of being possibly culpable, but I couldn't be sure who. I just knew that at least one of them had messed up big time and that he or they better step up and be a man about it and accept his punishment for the misstep. It couldn't point anyone out since I didn't know who was truly responsible and even if I did know, I wouldn't have said a word. That was the no snitching code that we all grew up with. You get caught, don't mention names, ever. If you did, your reputation would be soiled in perpetuity going forward and no one would want to deal with you. There was also an understanding that if you happened to be the sole cause of people getting jammed up, you did your duty and shouldered the burden so that others who were truly innocent didn't have to go down with you. That last part was apparently lost on whomever it was that got us arrested and later on detained. Some seem to think that if all just keep quiet, they won't be able to prove who is truly guilty and deserves the punishment, so they let all go free. Not taking into account the other outcome which is: sentence all of them since they all have some form of culpability. Those types of codes, I look at them as stupid now. Here is a code: be truthful and honest. How about that one? Sounds good to me. Back then the thinking was different though, this little abstract group we belonged to was for some reason worthy of our allegiance. When you later on sit there in the adult correctional facility and the letters don't show up any more, you make calls and the numbers are no longer active, the visitors that show up are your immediate family, that's when you realize what those codes are worth. Nothing at all.

It would be a rather long stay in pre-trial detention since a bunch of us didn't have anything to say, since we truly didn't know anything. And those who did, kept on refusing, satisfied with taking their chances in court and risking taking all their "friends" with them. Which is what ended up happening, we all went down. I suspect that the responsible individual/s was underaged and knew his sentence would be lighter if the court considered him guilty. Which one could argue would be an even greater reason to take responsibility for the mistake. Apparently he or they saw it from another angle. If we don't say a thing we might go free or get a mild sentence (mild in relation to what an adult would receive). As for the others involved in the case, excuse my language, F€%# 'em. And indeed, we got f----d. I got a year and a half, no more juvy, major league this time. At first I was really agitated and feeling some kind of way about it. Like many of us when we are locked up, we tell ourselves: this is the last time. That is what I was telling myself and those around me the last time I was doing time in juvy. I should have added in sha Allah at the end of that statement. Because truly, the only way to stay out of trouble is if Allah wills it. I was really disappointed in myself and at the same time really pissed off at those co-defendants who refused to clear the rest of us from this mess. We all got sentenced anyway, they should have just manned up and all of us wouldn't have gone down. My frustration with them did nothing to improve my situation and I realized that I had to start looking forward. After all it was my own fault that I was hanging out at the spot. Was there supposed to be those quantities of drugs there? No, that was the rule. Were there people coming through the spot all the time that were into all types of stuff that I really didn't want to have anything to do with any longer? Yes. I should have known better, the risk was omnipresent when hanging out with that crowd. They were really the only friends I (thought I) had though, it was either them or mom and sis. So as far as having any type of social life, that group was really all there was. I thought it was a case of being at the wrong place at the wrong time. Subsequently I would learn that there is no such thing as wrong place and wrong time, but in that moment that was what I believed. The stint in the adult prison would change my life dramatically. Both in a good way and in a very bad way. It ended up being the direct cause of me being where I am right now and having undertaken actions that I fear will doom me. It was also the cause of me truly finding God and being able to put my life and everything around me in a new context and it allowed me to in a way reset my frames of reference. One could say that it was a two-step process, one step towards the right direction and another one deep into the pits of hell.

Abu Salih

Walking into that prison I told myself, *this* is the last time. *For real* this time, in sha Allah. I remember looking around at the inside of that structure on my very first day and saying a silent prayer that none but me and God heard. *Please* Allah, let me get out of this place and never return! I was without a doubt nervous as I was entering the facility. I could sit here and act all tough when I write about it right now, but what good would that do? Give you a slightly tougher image of a guy that will already be dead when you read this? I'd rather be raw and honest and do my best to give you a genuine picture of myself. Even though I was used to institutions and knew more or less what to expect in there as far as routines go, the fact that this was on a new level, in combination with all the scary stories you heard about the pen over the years, put quite a bit of fear in my soul. In pretrial detention it was no big deal, I didn't think too much about it. My attitude was basically that I will deal with it when I get there. Out of sight out of mind kind of thing. When we rolled up towards the gates and I saw the facility in its full imposing grandeur, that's when it hit me, like a slap in the face. It was for real now. Chain link fences with barbed wire surrounded the entire colossal concrete structure. I remember just thinking: damn! Some people are doing life in here and will *never* get out. Well, in a casket they will. The doom of the whole situation was sobering, thank God I could find solace in knowing that I would be out in roughly a year. If everything went relatively well that is.

The inside of the facility was even more depressing than

the outside. I quickly realized that the place was *huge*, the earlier places I had been to didn't even compare. It was almost like comparing a kindergarten to a university. The first thing that hit me was the mood. Don't get me wrong, the mood was never great at the group homes and at juvy, but at least it wasn't a "I'm sick of life and sick of living" type of ambiance. Which is the type of energy that most people in this place seemed to emanate, at least in the unit that I was first placed in. At first I thought all units were like the one I first put my foot in, but soon I was informed that the one I was in was one of the worst ones one could find oneself in. Actually *the* worst, if we take "the hole" out of the equation. The hole was solitary confinement. Not an actual hole in the ground, but it might as well have been. It was reserved for the worst of the worst. It was a small cell, smaller than the standard one-man cells and it had a metal door without a window, only a slot that was big enough to fit a tray of food. The ones that were sitting in the hole were confined to that little space for twenty three hours a day. They had an optional hour of fresh air each day which consisted of walking around a rather small concrete rectangle while looking up at the sky through metal bars. There was no human interaction for those inmates save for the short moments when COs would give them their food or come by to ask them a question about something. Their living conditions were more or less the same that we read about apparently existing in the super max facilities.

My unit was not even close to that bad, even though in my estimation it was bad enough since it was much worse than anything I had encountered prior. Knowing that there was a worse place called the hole was of little solace. It more so existed as a boogeyman that was meant to keep one on relatively good behaviour. I knew then that the hole was not something for me to be really worried about. You basically had to do some serious shit to end up there. I came to that conclusion after seeing many inmates wilding out in my unit and not being moved anywhere. They were already at the second lowest rung on the ladder and were apparently not bad enough for the lowest one. I made it my mission to try to move up. The unit I was in was tough, in many different ways. The physical environment and the prevailing attitudes of everyone was tenacious and rough. I soon came to know that there were certain inmates in the very same unit that had been in the same cell for close to ten years now with no change of habitat. Again, that made me thank God that I wasn't supposed to spend much more than a year in there. Yet, a year in that unit seemed like more than a lifetime the way things were looking.

The unit consisted of several identical tiers. I happened to be on the second one. The rooms were small, really small. Perhaps like six by nine feet or something like that. I never got the exact measures, but I do know that it was well below the standard that the American Correctional Association called for. There obviously wasn't much in the room. A bed, a desk and a chair, all made of wood. A sink and a toilet bowl without a seat, both in lifeless stainless steel. There were three concrete walls and then the bars. Thick, dark, cold steel bars. Only to be opened by the COs. Anytime they wanted to walk by and see what you were up to they had a clear view of your entire cage. Nowhere to run, nowhere to hide. Many had the habit of tying up a sheet on the bars to get some privacy when nature called and one was forced to sit on the cold stainless steel to relieve oneself. I learned quickly that using some of the precious toilet paper as a toilet seat cover was worth it in order to not feel the toilet bowl directly on your skin. Putting up the sheet for that particular purpose was not frowned upon, but if the sheet stayed up for too long you would hear about it. "Cell C 12, take the sheet down!" If you didn't comply immediately they would pull it down for you and chastise you by hitting your bars with the batons just to mess with your eardrums. Some really tried to get away with having the sheet hanging there for extended periods of time. Some did it just out of the general principle that each human deserves his privacy, others had certain activities going on that they wouldn't do if it was possible for anyone to look into their cell. What that could have been I will leave to your imagination.

The inmates to the right and to the left of you basically became your quasi-cellies. They were the ones you could talk to after they locked the doors for the night. Many liked to use a little mirror that they would hold outside the bars so that the two people could make eye contact. That is not something that just looks cool in the movies. People actually do it in order to make the conversation more personable. Also, it is incredibly dehumanizing to deprive someone of being able to see the face of the person that you are talking to. Being able to at least lock eyes in a blurry mirror mitigates that feeling somewhat. Outside of the cells on the bottom tier was the open area where we all could socialize during the hours that we were not locked in. It was pretty sterile. Tables and chairs were anchored to the concrete ground in order for them to not be used when aggressions ran high. At some tables people socialized, at others they got their hair cut. Most of them were used for games of different sorts. Cards and dominoes were the most popular, followed by chess and backgammon. The only one I really cared for was chess. I had picked it up little by little in juvy. My brother used to mention to me that he played chess and I guess that spurred my interest. In juvy I was just trying to figure the game out and learn the basics. By the time I was done with juvy I knew how to play. I was very basic in my skill level but at least I knew how to get down. Or so I thought. The games they were playing at this place were on a whole different level. I tried my fortune a few times but got humbled in the worst way by guys twice my age. After that happened a few times I stuck to mainly just watching the heavy weights play. A good competitive game of chess was probably the best form of entertainment for me in there.

Some guys, believe it or not, hardly left their cells during the daytime. They preferred to stay locked in their cells. I'm sure they had their reasons. What they were, I have absolutely no clue about. I didn't necessarily mind my cell, but there was no way I would stay in the thing for an entire day without venturing out.

They also had some telephones out in the open area for us to use. Real old school payphones, the ones where you use the coins. Depending on how old you are when reading this, you might not even remember those existing out in society. We were allowed to make one call per day. Not long ones, usually ten to fifteen minutes was what they permitted. If the CO working the station that day was one of the cool ones, he might let you stay on for a longer while if there were not a lot of people waiting to use them. All calls were collect and had to be paid for by the recipient. I didn't use it too much honestly. I didn't have many to talk to on the outside. My brother was locked up in a different facility and the only two people I really cared for at home were mom and my sister. It sufficed to talk to them about once a week, and after a few weeks there is not a whole lot to say. They would update me if anything happened on the outside, which it rarely did. Mom kept on doing her thing while staying strong and my sister just kept on growing up at an alarming pace. As for friends, there was no one on the outside I cared to even talk to at that point. I had become completely disillusioned after we got busted and it was made clear to me that there was no honor in those (I almost wrote friendships) acquaintances. I knew there were still a few good ones out there. There had to be, right? At the same time though, it was close to impossible to know who was who amongst one's circle. And in addition to that, where had that social circle taken me? What had it done for me? Nowhere, nothing.

We also had yard time of course, for an hour each day we could get fresh air and get some physical activity in if we wished. There was a basketball court that was constantly full, with people on the sidelines waiting their turn to play. The games were short so that as many people as possible could play during that hour. What they lacked in length, they made up for in intensity. There was a general workout area where guys would lift weights and do dips and pull ups. Some guys got *huge* in there. And they got huge on a prison diet consisting of food that many first world countries wouldn't even classify as proper for domestic animals. I was never big on working out, it just wasn't my thing. I do remember looking at magazines when I was young with pictures of these guys looking like the Hulk. These workout magazines that told you how to lift, how to train. What supplements to buy, when to eat and what to eat. After seeing these guys get ripped in the yard my thoughts about those workout magazines could be summed up in two words: bull and shit. There was also a rather large patch of grass that was used for both soccer and football. Soccer seemed to be an exclusively Latin American sport in this institution, while football was dominated by the black inmates. Though much more inclusive than soccer, as football was one of those activities in prison that temporarily broke the ethnic barriers. Just because of that I used to like to watch it while getting my fresh air for the day. I never cared much for the sport, but I thought that the ethnic divides that existed in most of the institutions that I experienced were nonsensical. So seeing that praxis of segregation get interrupted during those games was somewhat of a thing of beauty in a place that for the most part manifested foulness. I mostly walked during our recess. Sometimes close to the walls, in what weren't circles since the yard wasn't round, but still constituting laps of some sort since I always ended up where I started. It was during one of those walks around the yard I met a person that would change my life completely.

Minding my own business one sunny day out there while walking along the wall, a young black guy approached me from the rear. He basically caught up to me and kept the same pace. I glanced sideways and saw a young-looking face, I estimated him to be about my age. A couple of years older, tops. I didn't really recognize him which must have meant that he was rather new. He didn't say anything so I didn't break stride and turned my gaze once again towards the direction I was walking.

"You are not from here, are you?" the guy asked me.

I thought to myself: from here? No one is from here, this a freaking penitentiary. I just replied that no, I was not.

"You are not American, I can tell. I mean, you might be from here. But you not really from here. You know what I'm saying? Your parents must be from the Middle East."

I must have looked at him with a weird expression on my face since he smiled back at me. People usually had a hard time placing me in the correct ethnic box. I usually heard such guesses as Puerto Rican, Domincan, Cuban, before the guesses took their course across the Atlantic. Then they would usually start out in northwest Africa before making their way further east. This guy hit it right away. I returned his inquiry with a question of my own and asked if he was West African. He sure had the looks. Super curly hair, dark skin, strong cheekbones. I had been around enough West Africans to recognize them when I saw them, I thought.

"Kind of like, but naw brother, I'm from here. Born on the East coast and so were my parents. My grandparents were from New York and Georgia respectively. I'm as American as a slave descendant can be. My name is Musa."

Ahmed, I replied as I was becoming a little perplexed as to why this African American guy presented himself with the Arabic version of Moses.

"Ahmed? I figured you were Muslim, something inside me gave me that feeling. Salam alaykum then."

He followed the peace greeting with a shining smile that exposed his ivory white teeth.

"Wa alaykumu salam wa rahmatullah."

That was our first interaction, the first of many. Recess was just about to be over and we walked inside together and took our seats at one of the chess tables that was not occupied. We sat down in silence, both knowing that we were about to have plenty to talk about. We locked eyes and the friendship commenced.

October 17th

This newfound friendship, this new camaraderie and above all brotherhood, would shape me tremendously over the next three or four months. We weren't the only Muslims in the unit, far from it. There were a good deal of brothers there, most of them were old enough to be our fathers and acted like uncles. The vast majority were African Americans and they treated Musa with endearment. As for me, they were cool with me but I sensed a distance that is hard to explain. They really did treat Musa like a nephew and little brother. With me it was different. It must have been my ethnic background that created the separation. I was still one of them in a way but I was not family, while they amongst themselves acted like one big family. It didn't bother me, it was just something I noticed. I had one real brother in there, that's all that mattered. That's all I needed.

We were on different tiers, me and Musa. So it was impossible for us to talk during the hours that we were locked in our cells. Instead we made the most of the time we could spend in the general area. We started having breakfast, lunch and dinner together. We walked during recess, he even got me to start working out for the first time in my life. I started doing push ups and burpees with this brother. He put me to shame since he was in much better shape than me, but he kept pushing me. From the beginning he told me that if your body is right, your mind will be right. Strong body, strong mind. They are interconnected, and so is the soul. If all the three aspects are strong and healthy, you will be a true human being. This is the type of wisdom that this guy who was basically the same age as me was dropping on me. I just liked listening to him, I liked asking questions and I liked just bouncing thoughts off of him. He was the only one in there that seemed to understand me and I believe the feeling was mutual. Outside of the ethic difference we were more or less the same person. Minority, grown up on the east coast, moved around, ended up in bad neighbourhood after bad neighbourhood. A few trips to juvy, bad circle of friends, unstable family structure, never understood the point of school, etcetera. And we were both Muslim. The thing that made Musa so different from all the other friends that I had up to that point, that more or less fit the same demographics, was that Musa had a type of depth to him. He also had what I can only describe as awareness. He seemed to be somehow in tune or always aware of God. In all our discussions, no matter what the topic, he would somehow bring it back to Allah and to Islam. In his mind everything was connected to this omnipresent power that was constantly dictating and influencing our affairs and matters on this earth. It could be big, great things. Or it could be small and seemingly insignificant things like the food we were served. Like the time I started complaining about something they claimed was fish which they served us for dinner one time. This one for some reason really sticks out. I started complaining about the terrible quality of the food and as soon as I was done with my rant about the correctional facility's cuisine Musa chimed in.

"Who do you think put it in their minds to serve us this particular dish today? You know the answer. It's Allah. It's all part of your test and your trial, and you are failing right now by complaining about something that He has decreed."

I couldn't muster a counter argument. If Allah was all powerful, how could these fools working in the kitchen go against His will? They couldn't, since that would in some way incapacitate Allah. The only reasonable follow-up thought I came up with was, why would Allah allow them to do this? Musa looked at me while chewing his food, pondering the query. He looked down on his food and made the fork fetch a good mouthful that he started chewing aggressively. His pearl-like eyes looked into mine. He had an answer, he always seemed to have an answer. After finishing the mouthful he was working on he laid it out.

"Allah lets them do this, and also lets other people do much more terrible things, in order for them to be part of *our* test that *we* are experiencing. And He also lets them do it so that they can manifest their own free will which He has given them. You get it? Their free will is doing this, since *He* lets them. And then He can punish them if He chooses to for their transgressions. While He will reward us if we are patient. But you brother, just failed the test by complaining about what you were served today. So repent to Allah."

The last line was followed by a laughter that came from deep down in the abdomen which when you heard, you had no choice but to join in on. That is how Musa was. Always profound and in the moment and at the same time relaxed enough to see the comedy in whatever it was that was going on around him. This attitude of his was very magnetic and it was hard not to be drawn to him, at least I thought so. He didn't seem to have too many friends in there, though he was cordial with quite a few inmates. I guess he just picked me as the one he thought was the most interesting of the people in there that he had things in common with. He had the mind of a mature person, that much was for sure, and at the same time he had this youthful energy and aura that I think would make it very hard for him to hang out with the older crowd for longer periods of time.

He told me about his history which had me scratching my head. At first I thought he was a young convert, which it turned out that he wasn't. Both his parents were Muslims, his father having passed away just less than a year before I met Musa. His father had died in prison, a fate I would never envy, much less so after seeing what this prison life was really about. So his parents were both converts, perhaps members of the Nation of Islam or something like that. I had heard enough about the NOI in the neighbourhood to be vaguely aware about what they were about and what they believed. He shot down that theory also and said both his parents had been born as Muslims. Ok, so who converted in the family? I had met many Africans that came from families that were completely Muslim, just like mine. Anywhere you looked in the family tree it was filled with Muhammads, Khadidjas, Alis, Umars and Fatimas. But an American from the South? This was unheard of. Both his grandparents on his mother's side had apparently converted after coming in contact with West African Muslims in New York City. That grandfather of his had been a well-known jazz musician who through his work came in contact with Muslims from the African west coast, apparently they were fairly prominent in the East Coast jazz scene. Musa's father's side of the family was different according to him. He claimed that they had all been Muslims ever since they were brought over as slaves from Africa. I know one thing about Musa, he was not a liar. That I know for sure, and he sounded convinced when he told me that part of his family's history. To me it sounded very far fetched and I thought he might be delusional about that part of his own history. I didn't call him out in it, but I did ask some questions regarding how that would even be possible. As always, there was an answer available and a rebuttal to my scepticism.

He pointed me in the direction of one of our many common areas of interest: books. We had read a little together before this particular conversation took place. I think maybe two or three books. Usually he would pick a book and we set a date when we both had to have finished it, then we discussed our ideas surrounding the book until they were exhausted. I can't remember exactly which books we read before this junction, one of them could have been To Kill A Mockingbird, but I'm not sure. A lot of books were read during the months we spent together and the order of them are not that clear in my mind. However, him telling me about his family tree and me questioning the narrative led him one day to hand me a book that I was not familiar with at all. It was Roots by Alex Haley. I was both captivated and fascinated by the book. I remember clearly that it took me on an emotional rollercoaster, it brought out a variety of sensations when I read it. Anger, laughter, sadness, disgust. It was all brought out of my core when reading Haley's pages. It culminated when it in the end explained what the entire chronicle was really about. At that point I also both understood and had a hard time comprehending why Musa wanted me to read the book. There had been Muslim slaves brought over to America in the transatlantic slave trade. This in itself was not completely new to me since it sounded at least vaguely familiar. The way the story was told explained the phenomenon in very vivid details, which I appreciated very much. The thing that confused and made me wonder why Musa wanted me to read the story, also made me confront him about the, in my eyes, flaw in his reasoning. Kunta was not able to pass on his religion to his descendants, not even to his own daughter. The only thing that remained of Kunta's faith, which he had arduously cultivated in his native Gambia, was stories about the mysterious practices of a grandfather from a far away land. After I made that point I realized that Musa had me right where he wanted me.

"That's right, Kunta was not able to pass his deen on. (Musa always used the Arabic word *deen* when talking about religion.) You saw how hard it was for him. But let me ask you something brother. How many slaves do you think were brought over to this country? I studied this bro. Probably over 10 million slaves were taken from Africa and around half a million of those ended up right here. That's what they say at least, I think that number is very suspect. Anyhow, a good percentage of those were Muslims, this we know for a fact brother. So Kunta wasn't able to pass it along, and the same happened with many others, obviously. But you can't tell me that out of half a million there wasn't a good amount that were able to pass it along even though all the circumstances were against them. If a believer is strong enough and determined, Allah can help him with what others deem impossible. Do you doubt that?"

No, I couldn't doubt that. If you have the All-Mighty on your side, who was going to stop you? It was still kind of hard to believe his story, but I had to admit that the reason I felt that way was that I was completely uneducated on the subject. He made a good case and I at the very least had to accept it as plausible. Such was the interactions with Musa, constantly he would challenge your mind and many of your preconceived notions.

He wasn't a preacher, far from it. Everything that was said, including the deeper philosophical points that he used to make, were all made in the flow of everyday conversation. He was quickly becoming the most interesting friend that I had ever known. There were some friends I'd been close with on the outside, but the more I thought about it, it dawned on me how incredibly superficial those acquaintances were. There were basically never any conversations about anything with real depth to it. It was drugs, girls, crime, complaints about whoever it was we didn't like, drugs again, crime again. Nothing about morality, nothing philosophical, no discussions about emotions. To a certain degree I understand that that was due to the environment that we lived in. We were trapped in a vortex of negativity and hate that clouded our visions to the point that we couldn't see much further than our own hand if stretched out in front of us, like an intense fog that engulfed the visibility of anything positive or profound. On the flip side, it's not like prison was a hub of love and peace. On the contrary. Yet, something about the sterile ambiance of the prison encouraged introspection. At least for the ones that were open to it. Those walls will do that to most people. That is when you realize that you are *all alone*. Except for, no one is actually *ever* alone. If you have an inclination to believe in a higher power, it will be invigorated by the circumstances of prison. If you aren't inclined towards that type of belief, at least prison will make you think about it in a way you never would have in free society. The next thing that happened to me was a natural progression to my newfound love for questions and discussion of the deeper variety. It would also be the main cause of my religious awakening.

Let me tell you all about it tomorrow. Nothing seems to be happening here on the ground that deserves your attention. If there is any action, I will let you know. For now, we are just holed up.

Me and Musa got called to the office of the supervisor of the unit we were in. It happened just like that as we were walking in from recess. A couple of COs approached us and told us to come along. We looked at each other perplexed, shrugged our shoulders and followed along. Most of the time when you get called to the supervisor it is a bad thing. Sort of like getting called to the principal's office in school, the reason just can't be a good one. On our way there we were both trying to figure out what this was all about. We were some of the best behaving inmates at the entire complex if you asked me. All we did was work out, read books, have conversations and occasionally I would be humiliated on the chess board. That was about it. Musa moved around a little bit more than I did, but was always discreet and on good behaviour. Neither one of us could figure out what this was about. At the same time, no need to fight it. Especially not when you can walk in there with a clean conscience knowing that you haven't done anything wrong.

The supervisor smiled at us as we stepped into his office. He signaled for us to sit down in the chairs that were waiting for us across from his desk. The two COs also entered the room but remained standing against the wall after closing the door to the office. The supervisor started complimenting us on our behaviour and also talked about how he heard good things about us from the COs and from other inmates. Both of us had absolutely no idea where he was going with this until he got to the point where he started talking about a room being open in another unit within the complex. Apparently there was a shortage of cells. (I know, very surprising when we are talking about the American prison system. The solution: build more!) It turned out to be the case that there was a different unit where inmates were cellmates and shared a cell. They needed a lot of the single cells for new inmates that were waiting to be placed at the facility and wanted to move us to the other unit. They were basically shuffling the deck of cards. Me and Musa looked at each other and thought: cool! Why not!? We accepted the proposal (by the way, if we had rejected it then the proposal would have turned into an order real fast) and the supervisor seemed very pleased with that. We had made his job easy by just going along with his idea. Other inmates would have fought the decision until they ended up in the hole, just to prove the point that they were sick and tired of taking orders from people that they perceived as some sort of overseers. We just looked at it like, why not? We enjoyed hanging out and we had heard good things about the unit we were to be taken to. On top of that, just a change of scenery was not a bad idea after roughly three months in the same place.

The unit turned out to be alright. It was still the same yard as before, the different units had different yard times. The general area was more or less the same. Different aesthetics, which was a welcome sight after the same desolate environment day after day. The routines were also more or less the same. Food, shower, yard, visits, phone calls. It was all the same, the only thing that changed was the schedule. The big difference was the living quarter. It was slightly bigger and had a concrete bunk bed. Same boring table and stainless steel toilet and sink. Sharing the toilet with someone while not being able to hide for privacy took some time to get used to. If there is one thing that I have learned about humans though, it is that we adapt. The unthinkable becomes bearable and the bearable becomes normal. All you need to achieve that is enough time. Me and Musa developed a timeout system. You called timeout and you had your uninterrupted time on the bowl. No conversation was allowed and the person not taking care of business was to remain doing what he was doing when the timeout was called. It worked remarkably well. The COs were different in the new unit. Generally speaking, they were a pain in the ass. I liked the routines better in the new place, but the COs were way worse. There were one or two that were alright and easy to deal with, the rest were trying to push our buttons. It didn't affect me and Musa too much. He always kept his head cool, somehow, some way. That coolness was contagious, indeed, his entire state of mind was very contagious. If it wasn't for his company I would have flipped out many times over. Not over any one thing, moreso as a result of an accumulation of many small provocations. With Musa as a companion, it was as if I was protected from the negative energy that was emanating from most of the COs and many of the inmates.

When I started sharing a room with brother Musa, that is when he started to really impress me. Up until that point I had seen a lot of him, but never truly up close. I knew that he used to pray with the older Muslim brothers, the "uncles." Up until the moment that we moved in together, our relationship mostly consisted of great conversations, workout sessions and eating together. In the evening he went to his room and

I went to mine. In the morning we would reemerge and continue where we left off the day before. In my short life I have learned two things about getting to know people and that is that you *really* get to know someone when you either travel with them or live with them. You get that up close and personal look that is so authentic that the person can't hide aspects of themselves even if they try their best. When you are in close proximity to someone in that manner, especially if it is for an extended period of time, enough strenuous situations will occur that will bring out the real selves of the people involved.

I mentioned it before, but it's worth reminding you since it is essential when trying to understand my relationship to my religion. Where I came from, religion was all talk, no action. Amongst my friends that is. Mom was religious, just like other old people were religious. Our generation liked to *talk* about our faith, but when it came to getting down to business and actually practicing and doing the deeds that we had talked about, a million excuses miraculously appeared and presented a convenient escape. Musa had much more substance to him and his thoughts were profound. You could tell by his delivery of his words that it was more than just rhetoric. That much was obvious after talking to the guy a few times. When we started living together his stature rose like helium in my estimation. This guy actually prayed (I know, this sounds stupid. I was impressed by a Muslim that was actually performing the prayers that we all believe are obligatory. My incredulity was based on my previous experiences though, so please forgive me) and he prayed all his prayers, on time. I had never witnessed this before from a peer and the brother instantaneously transformed from an impressive youth into a saint, right before my very eyes as I beheld his religious observance.

The guy would set his alarm and get up while the entire cell block was still in deep sleep, yours truly included. He would shut the alarm off quickly as he woke up, he was not one to spend unnecessary time in bed when there were more important things to do. The water running in the steel sink would momentarily pull me out of my slumber as he was getting ready for the dawn prayer. My habit in those early days of living with him was to go back to sleep as he was standing, bowing and kneeling on his prayer rug as the daylight was making its first presence felt outside the concrete walls of the prison. The very first time I was not even really understanding what was going on. That is how far removed I was from the religion my parents had handed down to me. My first thought was that this is a strange guy that sets his alarm in order to use the toilet in the middle of the night. As the days moved along I started to understand that this was not a hobby of his or just a topic of discussion. It was the nucleus of his very being. Without it, there would be no Musa. He would perform the prayers whose times fell during the time of day when our cells were open either in our cell or with the uncles in an area that they used to congregate at. Some of those older brothers would pray together in a part of the general area that had become accepted to be theirs, and no one in that unit had any objections to that. After we retreated to our cell as evening arrived, Musa would do the late prayers in our room, facing the concrete wall at an angle. It was also his habit to sit down and read the Quran after he had finished praying. He had this huge copy that was his most prized possession. It had the Arabic on one side of the page and the English translation on the other. He would read a verse in Arabic out loud and then follow that with reading the verse translated into english silently. I wouldn't say that he had the most melodious voice when he read, but nonetheless his recitation would take you into a trance if you focused on it. He was putting me to shame. Here was this African American guy reading God's word in pure Arabic while I, his cellmate whose parents' native tongue was Arabic could not even form words with those beautiful letters in his book, written in the finest calligraphy. It made me feel… I don't know if humiliated is the right word. But I was in some way ashamed when I noticed that this guy knew so much more about our religion than I did and that he also used that knowledge by actually practicing our deen. It was wake-up time for me. Literally and figuratively. As I saw Musa doing his routine day in and day out, it weighed down my conscience more and more each day. He was never bugging me about it. On a few occasions he asked me if I wanted to join him in prayer and a couple of times he reminded me that as Muslims, this prayer was not optional. In the beginning I was afraid since the truth was that I had completely forgotten how to perform the prayer and on top of that I suffered from what according to my own diagnosis was acute hypocrisy. I thought of all the dirt I had done in my life and the immorality that I had been a part of that was contrary to what our religion taught us. It felt like I was being inauthentic if after having all of that as part of my life, I was now all of a sudden going to stand there in prayer with someone as pious as Musa. That was the thing that was really holding me back. Deep inside I really did want to join him but was prevented by this excuse that I had built up in my mind. An excuse courtesy of the devil no doubt, who hates nothing more than a person getting closer to his Maker. The more I saw Musa pray, the more torn I felt inside. I knew that I *should* be doing what he was doing and my made-up psychological justification for not joining him was getting weaker and weaker by the day, but it was still there in the back of my mind. The devil was using the guilt that he knew I had over my past to prevent me from moving forward and leaving that life of immorality behind me. This was an ongoing struggle within me that existed for a few weeks. It got to the point where it started bothering me so much that I just had to choose a path. Either I would get even closer to Musa and try to walk the path he was treading or I would have to distance myself from him and forget about this whole spiritual thing because it was weighing too heavy on my conscience. I knew I needed guidance when it came to how to deal with this predicament and the best person to ask was also the one I trusted the most, Musa.

He smiled at me when I mentioned my spiritual plight. It was the type of sunny day where the sky is completely void of clouds, not even a speck of white up there. At least not from the vantage point from within the concrete walls, which in fairness to the absent clouds, limit the gazes of the inmates. We were sitting on one of the rare patches of grass that the yard had to offer, having just finished a few sets of burpees. We had both caught our breaths after the high intensity workout and our conversations started moving in the direction of the spiritual, which it very often did. I tried to open up the best I could when explaining the internal crisis I was experiencing. It was hard to put into words and I feared that my poor explanation had missed the mark by quite a lot. I took his smile as confirmation that what I had just said must have sounded strange and kind of spaced out. Instead it turned out to be the opposite.

"I know exactly what you are talking about bro. Most of us go through that at some point, it is totally natural. People that grow up like us and experience the types of things that we know happen in our neighbourhoods… we all go through it to some degree when we start practicing our deen. Some have a worse case than others. The ones that have always had some kind of level of religious practice in their lives usually have an easier time. The ones that are completely out of tune with Islam and then try to find their way back to the truth after having lived a life filled of immorality, they can go through it in a pretty bad way."

So yeah, me basically, I thought. The latter category was the one that I knew I belonged to.

"I call it PTHS. You will need counseling to get through it."

He laughed at his last remark as I was trying to figure out what he was talking about, it sounded like he had just diagnosed me with something that sounded like an STD. All I could do was ask him, what is it that you say I have?

"PTHS, post traumatic hood syndrome. It is the syndrome that afflicts you as you are approaching your true identity as a Muslim and are trying to clense your being from all the negative influences of the neighbourhood you grew up in. It can take some time to get through it, but you will, in sha Allah."

I felt a great comfort in hearing that he understood where I was coming from. Apparently I was not alone in experiencing this tug of war within my chest between my sinful past and aspiring present condition. He explained it further:

"This is all a trick of Shaytan. There is nothing he hates more than when a soul turns away from sin and sets its sight on God. So when that happens, the devil will use every single trick in his bag to derail the pursuit of truth and happiness for the seeker. One of his favourite instruments is your own conscience. He knows how to manipulate it and use it against you. Your conscience is a two edged sword, it can cut your opponent but it can also cut you. Your conscience can propel you forward and up to unimaginable heights but it can also hold you back from prospering if you let Shaytan manipulate it. And what Shaytan will do is use your guilt over your past to make you feel ashamed when you approach God. He will make you feel disgusted with yourself and dirty when you try to put yourself in the presence of people whom you look at as purified. It's all a trick though. We *all* carry dirt, bro. We all do. If all of us thought about it that way, that we couldn't pray with others because we have sinned, we can't fast because we still have sinful habits, we can't go to the masjid because we have some hypocritical tendencies, then *no one* would go to the masjid and pray. All the mosques would be empty, everyone would have a reason not to try to approach Allah. You know what I'm saying?"

I did know what he was saying. Everything he said was on point, as he was a psychologist with mind-reading capabilities. He had gotten to know me pretty well over the short time we had spent together, but I never imagined that he knew me *that* well. Or perhaps he didn't, perhaps these feelings that I was experiencing and he was describing were much more widespread than I could ever imagine. No matter what the case was, my next problem was to find out how I could get out of this satanic trap and somehow walk the path that my brother Musa was travelling on. I'm not even going to ask you to try to figure out where I found my answer.

"Look bro, you just have to *do* it. You have to force yourself in the initial stages. Like with most things in life that are acquisitional, this state of being has to be achieved through a struggle. It won't just be handed to you. The vision that you get, which you have already received, the insight that you are experiencing that is prompting you to even ask me this question, *that* is a gift from Allah the Most High. But the actual work, *you* have to do that. No one else can. And it is that very same work that will bring you closer to Allah and He will also reward you for it immensely in the next life. But it will require a tremendous struggle on your behalf.

You've seen that big black guy in the yard? Kareem, they call him. That dude, his arms are bigger than your waistline. How do you think he got that way? It all started with a thought, a thought that motivated him to start working out in order to get fit. Then, after the thought, the hard work began. He has been doing his workout routine in that yard for years now and he is the swollest brother in the joint. He achieved his goal. In the same way, you can achieve yours brother. You have to set your sight and then just go to work. And if you really want to do this then you need to start *now*. Don't let the devil play you by suggesting that this can wait until tomorrow, or that it can wait until next week. Or that it can wait until you are released from this place. I have heard stories about people procrastinating. I will never forget a story I heard about one brother. My uncle told me about him. This guy converted to Islam when he was like twenty three or twenty four. He took his shahada when he was basically our age. The guy died when he was twenty seven, and the tragic thing about it is that in the years following his shahada he never once learnt how to pray. He never went to the masjid. He kept on delaying and delaying, thinking that he would get serious with his deen later on in life. I guess he figured that he had many years left to live his raunchy life and that he would get serious when he was a little older and he didn't have his youthful energy any longer. Then death came to him when he least expected it. So he passed away without having ever stood in prayer with his brothers. Will Allah accept him? We don't know. We can only worry about ourselves in that regard. It will be a grind, but I will promise you right now that I will assist you on the way as long as we are connected."

He told me all the things I needed to hear. He was making sense while answering the questions that had been circling around my inner self. The urgency of it all really struck me. I couldn't lie to myself. The story he told about the guy who never prayed a proper prayer felt close to home. Many a time I had played with the thought of becoming religious in old age, but who is guaranteed old age? The fate of that guy seemed wretched and would be a nightmare scenario for anyone with an ounce of religion in the being. Musa was right in all he said. The time was now and the place was here. I had to take a hold of it. But how?

"If you feel ready, we start after lockdown tonight. I never forced you to do anything, right? But I can tell that you want this, so let's get to work today."

I was feeling shy for the first time since I was a child. I didn't even know the very basics of how to pray. I vaguely remembered something about washing in preparation for the prayer. Other than that, all I had was visuals of my mother kneeling on a prayer rug in our old living room. I was basically going to have to start with 1 + 1 and work my way up. The positive thing was that I had a teacher that seemed to know calculus.

That same evening after they had locked our doors we got started. It felt like some sort of initiation process. As if I was going to go through some ritual that would open the doors to a secret society that only a select few know about. I didn't actually believe this of course, I knew that I was already a part of the world's second largest religion and that I was on the cusp of becoming one of those that struggled hard to live up to the lofty standards that this faith demanded from its followers. Still, the aura of the moment was filled with mysticism and lofty expectations.

Musa started by showing me how to do the ritual cleansing that was required before the prayer. This might sound corny but I have to try to express it in a way that does justice to what I felt when I witnessed it. Him performing the ablution as a demonstration for me was a majestic sight. The way the water flowed over his dark limbs and his manner of stroking the water to make sure his skin became completely covered in water was a sight that could only be described as spiritually sublime. The moment felt hallowed despite the profane setting consisting of lifeless concrete walls and the dull stainless steel of the sink. I watched him closely and as soon as he was done I stepped up to the sink and repeated each element of the ritual with carefulness while Musa was observing me attentively to make sure I was doing it correctly, while droplets were still falling from his face and fingertips. He gave me a nod of approval when I was finished and it appeared that I had copied him in a satisfactory fashion. He took one of his towels and laid it out on the floor at an angle towards one the corners in the room. next to it he laid out his personal prayer mat and motioned for me to stand on it, to the right side of his towel. He took his place to my left, about half a step in front of me.

"Just follow my movements. I know you don't really know how this is done, so we are going to keep it simple. Follow me the whole time. You don't have to say anything, just pray with your heart. Alright?"

Alright. That is all I did, I followed him every time he shifted positions in the prayer. When we were standing he recited the

Quran beautifully while I stood there trying to pick up singular words I could understand from this dialog with Allah. We went through all the progressions of the ritual until we knelt for the last time and put our foreheads on the ground. That is when the floodgates open for me. Tears exited my eyes and I was completely incapable of holding them back. I must have only spent about fifteen or twenty seconds with my face prostrated on the mat that was covering the concrete floor, but it could just as well have been a lifetime. All the shit I had done up to that point in my life was displayed for me on the inside of my closed eyes. All the mistakes, all the hurt, all the pain. It all showed itself in that one moment and I relived it all in a span of a few seconds. Directly following that, I realized that the only way to leave all of that behind and make amends for it was to do what I was doing in that very moment with Musa. I had never felt closer to God in my entire life than when I was prostrating myself next to my brother and teacher. I realized in that point of time that what I was experiencing was God's mercy manifesting itself. It was as if God had opened a door and invited me in. All I had to do was take a few steps. I knew I had found what I was looking for and I was instantaneously thankful that I had a guide like Musa who could lead me through that door. The dawning of the realization upon me made it impossible for me to control my emotions and flowing tears was the only natural response. Throughout what was left of the prayer I kept on crying, as silently as I possibly could since I did not want to disturb Musa whom I could sense was in a state of deep concentration. He finished the prayer with greetings of peace to his right side and then to his left. I followed suit and realized I had just completed my first prayer as an adult. We sat still on the floor in silence for a while. Or rather I sat in silence while Musa was almost soundlessly pronouncing what I would later on realize were praises and magnifications of Allah. He looked at me when he was done.

"Alhamdulillah. You did it brother. You felt it, huh?"

Yes, I did definitely feel it. I knew that there was no turning back from this. I had entered the door with the help of Musa and now I was on the inside. After feeling what I had just felt I was certain that whatever this was that I had encountered was what my soul had been searching for unknowingly for many years. We all look for satisfaction, satisfaction of different sorts. That is the mission that man is undertaking while roaming this earth. Some look for it in money, some in possessions, status, fame, notoriety, power. The list is too long to complete. What I know now is that *true* satisfaction will never come from those worldly things, they hadn't for me and they never will for anyone else. Real satiation and contentment can *only* come from He who created us. We are body and soul. You can try to satisfy your body as much as you want with the luxuries of this world but the soul will still be craving satiation. As long as that does not happen our beings will be in a state of imbalance that is not conducive to being satisfied and happy in the true sense. By establishing a relationship with the Divine this balance can be achieved and one's entire being can find succour. I had never felt that harmonious state until that very moment, but as soon as I did, I knew that I wanted to strive to feel it again. Even if I wouldn't, the pursuit in itself would be the path that I chose for myself.

With this newfound bond that was founded on religious practice, our friendship rose to a higher level. From that evening when I prayed with Musa for the first time, I never missed a prayer as long as I was by his side. The majority of the five daily prayers we prayed together in the room. At times, when a prayer time fell during the hours that we were not constrained to our cells we would pray separately. If I was by myself or in the company of someone other than Musa, then I would just retreat to our cell and perform my prayer there. During the daytime Musa would often hang out with the uncles, the older African American Muslims. He spent increasingly more and more time with them as the weeks moved along, never at the expense of our time together. I felt that he prioritized me throughout our time together in prison, but the time he spent with the elders rose incrementally with time. I'm not really sure why that was the case since I got the sense that he did not enjoy their company all that much. He took me with him to the area in which the uncles used to congregate. They had part of the general indoor area that had basically been made theirs. They used to pray out in the open in a rather large group. On a couple of occasions I went there with Musa and prayed with them. They couldn't reject me since I was there for the purpose of bowing and prostrating myself with them to the God that we all believe in. Truth is that I never really felt welcomed. After we had prayed, no one even pretended that they were interested in interacting with me. As soon as I felt those vibes I understood that there was no point in tagging along with Musa to that place in order to pray. With Musa, religion was *never* racial. It was all about the soul and its purpose in this world. He understood that our physical attributes were in a sense totally arbitrary from our point of view since none of us chose our skin color, or hair color, or the color of our irises. We didn't choose our parents or in which country we were born and we didn't decide which language would be spoken in the household we grew up in. All these facets of our beings were completely out of our control and in the mind of Musa they were utterly inconsequential to our place in Islam. I agreed wholeheartedly with his idea about this matter. Unfortunately that did not seem to be the case with the majority of the uncles. For them there seemed to be a racial aspect to Islam that I could never quite figure out why it was necessary. Musa had explained to me the vision that the Prophet Muhammad had and how he was always ready to accept new converts, no matter what their background might be. He told me a story of one of the last public speeches that the Prophet gave, where he proclaimed that the Arabs did not have any superiority over the non-Arabs and vice versa, and that the white man did not have any superiority over the black man, and vice versa. The only thing that determined a person's greatness vis a vis other people was the level of piety and mindfulness of God that the person possessed. This all made sense to me as this would place all humans on a level playing field when it came to approaching God through righteous deeds. By feeling the attitudes of the uncles I realized that they did not necessarily share this perspective fully. It didn't bother me too much. My newfound religiosity was sufficient for me and Musa's company was plentiful as far as companionship was concerned. Musa nonetheless spent time with the uncles on a regular basis. They really seemed to like him and I assume that they felt some kind of parental responsibility towards this young brother who they might have thought needed protection and guidance in that rough environment. I never got the sense that Musa was crazy about hanging out with those older brothers, I think he did it more out of a feeling of reverence towards that older generation of Muslims who without a doubt wanted what was good for him.

We had a discussion about destiny one day in the yard. I remember that it was an off day for us in our training regimen, so we sat on top of a bench with our feet resting on the wooden beam that is meant to sit on. A very normal posture in hoods worldwide I would assume, when your butt is on top of the backrest and your feet on the seating surface. The sun was beaming that day, though it wasn't really that warm. I tried to soak up as many rays as possible with my face, having realized that any moment the sun and I were out simultaneously was an important moment for my health. The weeks and now months of limited exposure to the sun and fresh air was starting to show its signs on me. I was becoming pale and my skin was starting to break out in a way it had never before. I wasn't the only guy with those types of symptoms in prison and realized that many of us suffered from sunlight deficiency.

While absorbing the sunshine during that recess I started talking to Musa about destiny and how we should view it. I had recently, not long after I started praying, realized that coincidence and random chance was something that I could not subscribe to as controlling my life. I started to view my own existence and also my surroundings as completely purpose-driven. The spiritual station I had reached and which filled me with new life was a direct consequence of the situations I had gone through. In other words, I could not see myself in that position if it wasn't for meeting Musa and also going through everything that led to me being locked up in that particular facility. That realization had been dawning on me for a period of time as I became immersed in my new religious identity. I told Musa that as I got arrested, then sentenced and finally placed at this facility, I thought that this was due to me being in the wrong place at the wrong time. From a purely materialistic perspective this did seem to be the case, but for someone with a deeper perception, that type of explanation was only an easy way out and a means for avoiding any theological implications.

"Listen my brother. Chance, randomness, coincidence, fluke… whatever they want to call it. It's a way to try to cover up the obvious fact that there is a Planner behind all of this. Just look at the world, look at nature. So many things are in perfect order, there is so much harmony. Only us humans mess it up, we are the ones that destroy that beautiful balance. It is clearly a design, whoever denies that does it at their own peril. The same holds true for our lives and the paths we take. Just think about all that had to happen for your parents to meet, which then led to you being born. Or for my parents to meet, if they didn't I certainly wouldn't be here talking to you right now. Then you think further back, imagine all that had to happen for our grandparents to meet, which led to our parents existing. And our great grandparents, and so on. It goes back innumerable generations. If just one of those couples never met due to whatever minute reason we can conceptualize, then me and you would not be here right now. But we are here right now, so this is the only real outcome. That means that what transpired before us *had* to happen. Just like what preceded us meeting in this place *had* to happen. People often say what you just said: I was in the wrong place at the wrong time. Let me tell you, there is no such thing. You were at the right place at the right time. What's important is: being in the right state and the right mind."

I will never in my life forget that line from Musa. I mean, it will be inconsequential shortly when this life of mine is over, but since the moment he said it I never stopped pondering it. It has always been in the back of my mind. He continued:

"If your mind is in the right place and your soul in its natural state, *nothing* bad can happen to you. That is so because if you are in that proper state and in tune with Allah, then you will realize that everything that befalls you comes from Him and none else. I mean, things can happen that you yourself were the cause of, or perhaps someone else did something to you. Regardless, even those things happen with Allah's will. Who else gave those people the ability to try to do that thing to you, you know what I mean? The two dimensional mind only sees cause and effect in this material world, but the three dimensional mind can see the cause existing on a different plane. When that happens, that is when you realize that *everything* that happens to you is from Allah and it is a part of your individual test. With that frame of mind comes acceptance and with acceptance comes tranquility and satisfaction. Afterwards comes the realization of purpose. You are seeing that now, I can tell. We both have benefitted from finding each other here. But there would be no *us* if it wasn't for what came to pass prior to all of this."

I had a hard time understanding in what way Musa was benefitting from my company, to me it looked like a one way street. A teacher and an ignorant student. I'm sure he would have a clever answer in store for me if I asked him that question. There was no real need to ask it though. I was getting everything I could have asked for from our acquaintance and if he claimed to also profit somehow from our friendship, who was I to question that?

It didn't take long before praying regularly felt natural to me. In the very beginning I experienced the reoccurring times of the prayer each day as, not exactly tedious, but it took a lot of effort for me to get used to the regimen. That was probably a result of me living in a very unstructured way for most of my life. Having steady routines took some time getting used to, but the more acquainted I became with it the better I started feeling. I don't think that it was just the routine itself, since I already had a form of routine before that in my dealings with Musa. We used to work out, hang out, walk. On top of that, the institution itself was based on a life that consisted of nothing but patterns and habits. Which I did not mind in and of itself. The fact that things were organized felt good, I had noticed that it fit my personality better than the spontaneous type of approach that I always had on the outside. The big difference now though was that my new routines had a greater purpose. I wasn't doing things according to a specific pattern so as to achieve some form of order. Instead the pattern was now connected to a higher spiritual purpose. There was not just some sort of worldly material benefit, there was also a kind of nonmaterial benefit when taking on this devotion. I slowly became addicted to it. The more I did it, the more intense my sense of tranquility was becoming. It felt like I was naturally drawn to it in some way, as if my soul had found something for which it had been longing for a long while without really knowing it.

After a few weeks, me and Musa were not only praying together but also doing other things to strengthen our faith. Slowly he had started to teach me how to read in Arabic. It took a *lot* of practice and patience to learn the letters and then to put them together to form words. Fortunately for me, alhamdulillah, I was familiar with the sounds and could pronounce the letters without any real difficulty. My reading was extremely shaky in the beginning but everyday it improved by small increments until I could make my way through the text of the Quran while struggling. Musa read fluently, at least it sounded like flowing water in my ears. He admitted that he did not understand everything that he read. I sure couldn't tell by the sound of it, but according to him he understood about thirty percent of what he laid his eyes on.

He tried to push me to lead the two of us in prayer. I was extremely reluctant to take him up on this suggestion. First of all, I knew that he was *way* more knowledgeable than me and I was really scared of messing up out of nervousness if I was to lead him in prayer. Secondly, I viewed myself as a big sinner. Musa was no doubt closer to God than me and the probability of our prayers together would be accepted must have been exponentially higher with him being the imam, the one leading the prayer. He did his best to diffuse my concerns by saying that in the view of Allah we were all the same. Musa claimed to also be responsible for innumerable transgressions and that he was in no better position than me to present our prayers to our Creator. No matter which way he tried to argue, I just couldn't do it. I was still very ashamed of my godless past and embarrassed by my own lack of knowledge. Next to Musa I felt like a child next to a wise teacher, and spiritually speaking that was without a doubt the case. It wasn't until recently that I understood why he was pushing me to take on that responsibility. I think he did it partly in order to force me to develop within the religion by taking on a task that I was not at that point suited for. The bigger reason though, I believe was out of piety. The brother really did not hold himself in high estimation with his Lord. He was probably scared that his prayers would not be accepted. All I can say is that, if Musa's prayers are not accepted, then whose prayers are accepted? It seems strange, but I truly think that was the level of consciousness and fear of God that he possessed.

He also taught me how to fast. Fasting was, after the prayer itself, the thing that elevated my spiritual awareness and strengthened my faith the most. Ramadan had already passed before me and Musa got to know each other. We would have to wait for many months until it would return. Musa would talk about the month of Ramadan as if it was a beloved relative, or perhaps even a lover that was yearned after. Due to the uncertain conditions of life in prison there was no telling if we would have the pleasure to experience this sacred month together when it would arrive. So we did the next best thing, we undertook voluntary fast. At first I was apprehensive. To be honest, it kind of scared me. No food from dawn until sunset? And on top of that, no water, no coffee, no tea. I thought I was about to embark on a suicide mission (spare me the sarcastic eye roll) since I thought that there was no way that my body would be able to take it. Then I remembered that mom used to do it back home. She also used to go to work while fasting, come home and take a nap and then wake up and prepare her food that she would eat right after she had performed her sunset prayer. If my old mother could do it while at the same time working and worrying about me, my brother and my sister, then I should have absolutely no excuses in prison. Except for the schedule of the daily activities that was to be followed strictly, there was nothing about my circumstances that should make fasting harder for me. Sure, time moves slowly behind bars, but there were plenty of things to occupy oneself with if one wanted time to pick up its pace. Especially for a bibliophile like myself, there were always books to read. I came to the realization that my fears were unfounded and that the only thing holding me back was spiritual laziness and excuses courtesy of Shaytan.

The first day I tried it was a life-changing experience. I remember that it was a Thursday. Musa had told me that the Prophet Muhammad, peace be upon him, used to perform the voluntary fast on Mondays and Thursdays. So it seemed like a great day to try it out. We got up some thirty minutes earlier than we usually did for the dawn prayer that day. We went through our ritual cleansing after waking up and then sat down to drink a bottle of water each. We had some biscuits that we had bought from the commissary, as well as some fruits. This became our fuel for the day that was waiting to make its appearance with the light of dawn. We prayed together as soon as the time arrived and then we both sat for a short while reading the Quran. We both layed down for a short while as there was still plenty of time left before they would unlock the doors. I can't even remember if I slept during that time. I was mostly just laying in bed feeling profoundly relaxed, yet excited to walk upon a new path within Islam.

It is very hard for me to explain to you the feelings that I was experiencing when I was fasting. As that first day moved along all my previous fears of not being able to take the physical toll disappeared. I noticed that my energy level was more or less the same as it usually was. We even did a light workout in the yard that day, we didn't go as hard as we usually did just to stay on the safe side, but we still got it in. At lunch time we retreated to our cell while the other inmates ate. It almost coincided with the noon prayer which we prayed in our little abode. That prayer was different. Just like something supernatural happened the very first time I prayed with Musa, something special happened when I prayed that first prayer while fasting. Again, the feeling transcended words that I can put on this paper. The best way I can describe it was that I felt a type of closeness to the Divine that I had not felt prior. The prayer itself always made me feel near and with the element of fasting added on top of that it just made the presence that much more intense. While all the other inmates were going about their business as usual, me and brother Musa were walking around all day worshiping our Lord without people even knowing it. I realized that fasting was like a secret between you and God since no one else could truly know that you were fasting. Even if you told them they couldn't be sure since they are not by your side twenty-four/seven observing your every move. On the other hand, even in one's most private moments of seclusion, God is there in His knowledge, so tricking Him that you are fasting is an impossibility.

We skipped dinner in the dining hall since it also fell during the daylight hours. Instead we took our rations and snuck into the room and stashed it. That was forbidden under normal circumstances. The uncles had told Musa that they made an exception for the Muslims that are fasting during Ramadan, but we did not want to take our chances on a random Thursday. Since if they said no, we would be without a proper meal that day. Sneaking it in was worth the risk. That way we could eat properly after they locked the doors and the sun had set. We didn't have to wait too long to eat after they locked all the doors. It might have been like an hour or something, I can't really remember. We both prepared for the prayer by washing long in advance. I didn't have any real feelings of hunger at that time. They had come and gone during the day but my stomach was pretty numb as evening was approaching. Thirst was what was really getting to me, I had started to regret that little workout session around noon. We had a couple of bottles of water and a bottle of Coke from the commissary on chill. How do you chill something in a prison when you don't have access to a fridge? Please don't become disgusted. Even though I would not blame you if you did since that was my first reaction when I first saw it, but believe this: things that seem weird and perhaps also odious have a manner of becoming accepted and normal after long enough behind bars. We used the toilet bowl as a cooler. If the drinks were even moderately cold when you first got them, the toilet bowl with its rather cold water and steel exterior functioned as a better cooler than one would expect.

As the time for the prayer neared we busied ourselves with supplications and Quran reading. We both read in voices that were low, yet audible, but not loud enough for it to disturb the other person. Musa always had a great sense of time. It was almost as if clocks were superfluous in his world, an accessory for the vain whose actual function was already fulfilled by an internal timer. When fasting he was even more in tune than usual and kept an eye on the alarm clock in our room in between the pages he was reading. As soon as the clock hit the time we were waiting for he gave me a head nod. The nod meaning that it was time for me to stand up and chant the call to prayer. It had become our habit to do it that way, me calling it out, and him acting as the imam when we prayed. No one in our cell block seemed to mind. At that time of the evening the tiers were usually noisy. Television sets blaring out cacophony, radios blasting music and heated conversation making their ways out of numerous cells. As long as it wasn't unreasonably loud, the COs didn't care whatsoever. That meant that I could raise my voice a little while calling to prayer without anyone getting annoyed by it. The sound emanating from my throat would be drowned out by the noise level on our tier anyway and would probably only reach the cells closest to us. As soon as I was done with the call we sat down to drink and eat something very light before we performed the sunset prayer. Musa extracted the two water bottles from the toilet bowl and washed them meticulously in the sink. We emptied those water bottles swiftly in between bites of bananas and apples that we had stored in our room. Let me tell you, a bottle of water (straight from the toilet nonetheless) had *never* tasted better. We smiled at each other as soon as we had finished that modest breakfast and simultaneously exclaimed: alhamdulillah.

We stood up and prayed together, just like we did every evening at sunset. This time around the prayer was different though. It was as if I was coming down from the fasting high as we were standing, bowing and prostrating. All throughout the ritual I kept thanking Allah in my heart for letting me complete the act of worship that I had just performed from dawn 'til dusk. When we finished we sat down again on the floor where we had broken our fast and we pulled out the dinner that we had saved from earlier in the day. Musa uprooted the Coke bottle from the toilet, washed it, opened it and emptied its content into two styrofoam mugs we had in our room. I took out some cookies that I had bought earlier in the week and we had a feast. You might think this is hyperbole, but it might have been the best meal I had up to that point. It was a prison dinner that had sat in our cell for a few hours, with Coke and some stale cookies that you can probably find at the 99 cent store. To me, it could have been from your local five star restaurant, that's how good it tasted. I don't think I ever appreciated food in the same way that I did that day. We chatted until it was time for the last prayer of the day and then ate a little bit more before we went to bed. Before laying down I looked at Musa and told him that I wanted to do this again, the very next day. He smiled at me with his characteristic smile that he would paint his face with when he knew something that you didn't know.

"Brother, pace yourself. Our Prophet didn't fast every day, but he did it regularly. If you like this, it's a good thing. That means that Allah has opened a new door for you that you are ready to enter. But you have to measure your steps. I showed you this since you wanted it, but I won't let you burn out. That is the worst thing that can happen to someone that wants to get in touch with his religion. He gets a good taste of it and he just wants more and more and more. The thing is that your body and your spirit have limits when it comes to how much they can expose themselves to. Therefore, your pace needs to be steady. It doesn't have to be fast, the most important thing is that you are constantly making progress, even though it might be minuscule. That will be better for you in the long run than if you try to take too much on at this early stage. Just trust me on this one."

Trust him I did, even though I have to admit that it was very hard to take his advice in this instance. The level of consciousness I experienced while fasting was a type of high that I had never experienced before and I got hooked instantaneously. Dopamine levels must have been through the roof and I wanted more of it right away. The beautiful thing was that it was available each and every day if I wanted it. Or so it seemed at the outset at least. Musa's warning about burning out did make some sense to me. When it comes to highs, it is usually the very first one that hits you the strongest and you might end up on a never ending quest to recapture something that will forever be elusive. The pursuit itself can be a dangerous undertaking as the object of one's pursuit, the high in this case, might become an actual purpose, which it was not originally meant to be. In this case with the fast, or any other form or worship for that matter, the goal is not to feel some sort of metaphysical sensation. The purpose is the worship itself and recognizing who one is worshipping and what His rights upon us are. The spiritual trips that we might experience along the way are only gifts which God bestows upon the seeker in order to let His servant feel a fraction of the pleasure of what awaits him in the everlasting afterlife.

What I just put down are not my own thoughts about the matter. Well, they are now. I meant, they didn't come to me like that. The source was once again Musa. I basically paraphrased one of our many discussions on the subject. He was very keen on getting me to slow down. Which could not have been an easy task. My eagerness grew by the day and I felt that it would be hard to contain going forward. My ambition and zeal needed an outlet, I just didn't know what it could possibly be (later on I would know, and so will you if you haven't already figured it out). I assume that Musa also struggled to find what it could be that could serve as a release for my new passion. So the only way he could deal with it I guess was to try to harness me and my wild soul.

He did a tremendous job when it came to that. If Musa had not been there with me in that early stage I really don't know what would have happened. I would probably have tried some form of perpetual fasting and prayer routine that would have left me sleep deprived and eventually diagnosed and sent to infirmary. Now that I look back on it his presence and companionship was a major blessing . He was also smart enough to balance out our activities so that I wouldn't take the religious practice too far. At the time he kept on encouraging me to keep up my routines together with his. He could sense how important Islam had become to me in a very short time. Musa already understood what an enormous gift this religion is for whoever happens to receive it and to let it go to waste was not an option in his mind. Through his stories I heard of people who had squandered this precious favor granted them by God Himself. Either through not appreciating it enough and not giving it the respect and attention that it deserves, which led to them not treasuring it and losing it accordingly. Or people who were overzealous and went in on the deep end without even knowing how to swim in these unknown predator-filled waters and consequently drowning and never seeing the fruits of their quest.

He set out to make sure that I would not suffer either of those two fates. The job he did in that regard was remarkable. What happened after me and him got disconnected was not his responsibility and it was impossible for him to foresee. During the remainder of our time together he made sure to create a proper balance of religious and worldly activities. We kept up our prayers on a daily basis as well as our Quran reading. We fasted about once a week, that was usually the highlight for me, even though I could never quite recapture the sensation of that very first fast. We stayed dedicated to our workout routine, which was picking up in intensity. After a few months in Musas company I was without a doubt in the best shape of my young life, which I in hindsight understand also contributed to my spiritual well-being. It was as if the physical well being, the mental and the spiritual all went hand-in-hand. The fact that I felt that I was peaking in all three spheres at the same time was far from a coincidence.

One area where I never peaked, I would even say that my whole experience consisted of one long and deep valley, was the chess board. I kept on getting destroyed by those that had any type of experience with the game. It got to the point where some guys wouldn't even want to play me because they saw it as a waste of time, I didn't put up enough resistance. I found a few beginners that were close to my level that I could at least play some games against and the outcome was not a forgone conclusion. Something about the game captivated me even though I never even came close to even approaching proficiency in any way. The tactics and the planning was interesting to me. As well as the movements of the different pieces and the dimensions of the board. In chess, I figured that one could never blame anyone except for oneself if failing. There are no dice, no drawing of cards, no lucky or unlucky bounces. Everything was purely determined by your own decisions and those of your opponent. If you lost, you had to just accept it and move on, hoping to improve in order to win the next one. I found the combination of the predetermined rules and the volition of each player which led to the result of the game, a perfect metaphor for life. Some rules are in place when you are born, some of your conditions that you face are predetermined. What you make of them though and where you wind up is up to your own self.

The main non-religious activity that we spent a lot of time on was book reading, and discussions about those books. The library was packed with good stuff and they had a book club that met every week in the library. Hey, call me a nerd, a dork or whatever. I will just tell you that the conversations and discourses that we had in that book club were the deepest ones I had in my time in prison, outside of all the talks that me and Musa had in private. That book club was the only place I saw people from all different backgrounds sit down around one table and act civilized in each others' presence. Too often when ethnic lines were "crossed" and intermixing occured, it usually ended in negativity. Not all the time, don't get me wrong. There were plenty of people in there that enjoyed the company of a fellow inmate from a different background or of a different ethnic makeup. What was extremely unusual though was that many different ethnicities would gather at one place at the same time and act cordial. Which is just what happened in our little circle. We must have been around eight guys and a CO, if I remember correctly. Me and Musa of course. Then there was an Indian guy, Dheepak or something like that. Which was hilarious to us just because of the endless Tupac jokes we could come up with. We also had a Cuban, Macario. He was rather dark skinned and could easily be mistaken for an East African with his sharp facial features and grandiose disposition. I have never felt attracted to men (I know, the mandatory disclaimer) and I wasn't attracted to him either in any emotional sense. Still I have to say that Macario was one of the most stunning human beings I have ever laid my eyes on. We also had a Salvadorian kid, the guy claimed to be twenty-two but looked much more like fifteen. Nestor was his name. If his looks made him appear much younger than he was, his intellect made him seem much older. His mind was always alert and his perception savvy. Only

God knows all that Nestor had been through. My conclusion after interacting with him quite a lot was that whatever had happened in his past had made his mind develop far beyond his physical age, and perhaps also in some weird way stunted his corporeal development. There was also a big white guy in our group, Mike (yes, of course it had to be Mike. It's always Mike.). Mike had already read all the books we read in this circle, perhaps more than once. He was like an encyclopedia when it came to literature and he always had thoughts about the books we read that none of the others thought about. Zach was an African American that was a real character, to say the least. The guy was too smart for his own well being. He had many opinions and seemed to feel strongly about each and everyone of them. If he truly did or not, I don't know. One thing he did though was to argue as if each opinion he held was law. The truth was probably that he was just an argumentative person, he would argue anywhere he happened to be. In the yard, in the dining hall and probably in the cell (poor cellmate). Once we all understood what he was there for, we were able to look past his argumentative nature. It was never personal with Zach, he was just that type of guy. The fact that the guy was hilarious made his presence welcome, he was always the one bringing jokes to the table when the discussion became too stale. He also wasn't above making fun of himself from time to time. There was also an Asian guy, like far east Asian. I can't remember exactly where from, Cambodia or one of those remote places. This guy seemed really smart, his problem was that he struggled with English mightily. Not in the sense that he couldn't understand. He might have understood some of those texts better than the rest of us. It was just that he was limited when it came to expressing himself. On top of that he had a *major* accent that was really thick. He had ideas and thoughts that seemed deep but he had problems expressing them. It was almost painful to watch him struggle to extricate the words that existed on his inside in a foreign language and verbalize them in English. We all liked him though and let him be a part of the group, there probably wasn't a better way for him to improve his linguistics. The CO's name was Sanchez, Chez for short. He was one of the ones that was always cool with us. He wasn't one of us like the other guys in the group. This was just a natural consequence of him having a uniform on. Nothing personal, just the standard "us and them" mentality. He was a book nerd and really knew his stuff, no doubt about that. He was very clever but was smart enough to keep his distance. If he would have dominated the discussions too much we would have looked at him sideways and he was very aware of this. So he laid low and chimed in when it was fitting, careful not to talk more than anyone of the inmates at the table. There were a few other guys that came and went rather swiftly. They might have stuck around for a book or two, but not more than that. I can't even really remember their names quite honestly. The aforementioned was the core of the group though and we stuck together for close to six months I believe.

We took turns picking books. For some reason we all seemed to gravitate towards classics. Perhaps a couple of us started out picking classics and then it became some kind of subconscious theme that the entire group felt bound by. That is my guess at least. We went through a lot of rather famous books. We did Frankenstein, The Process, The Great Gatsby, Letters from the underground, 1984, the Count of Monte Cristo, Roots. The list is long, those are some of the ones that I can recollect right now. We also had some poetry books sprinkled in here and there in between the classics. I had started to appreciate poetry a lot while I was locked up. Poetry fulfilled a need for us that other types of literature couldn't quite do. The prison experience consists of so many surreal and abstract feelings and sensations that cannot really be captured by traditional prose. It can catch a lot of it and express it reasonably well but there are other things that are functions of the prison experience that can only be expressed accurately through the work of the poet. Therefore I think that many of us could relate to the world of metaphors and similes that many poets presented in order to convey their own perceptions of their experiences. They all led to deep and interesting discussions. Everyone brought their own perspective to the table and we were able to exchange thoughts about all these works and their authors. All the ethnic boundaries that would have existed in the dining hall or in the yard for example with this mix of people were nonexistent in that library once we sat down around that table and dissected literature. That book club became an escape for many of us since we could, in that group and during that time together, transcend the norms and expectations that were cast upon us in most other times and places in prison. We could be a version of our own selves that was much closer to who we felt we were in our essences, liberated from the correctional facility roleplay we were obliged to follow thanks to the prevailing prison culture.

The book club was one of the highlights of my stay in that prison. Probably the next best thing after the precious time

I spent with Musa. My time in the book club would come to an end, but not before my companionship with my mentor and teacher would. All good things in the world must end. This I have no problem accepting and I never really had at any point in my life. I had seen enough struggle to realize that pleasure in its pure form was not meant to be experienced in this life. Accepting tragedy was something I had grown used to. The hard part was accepting the *way* tragedies occurred and the *reason* for them befalling me. It is hard for me to express what Musa meant to me, though I have given it my very best try while writing what you have just read. These words are not enough though and much will remain unsaid, that is the nature of emotions and experiences. I truly believe with conviction that Musa was sent by Allah to me to save me from my heedless existence and bring me into the light of truth. A truth which I saw with my own two eyes and felt within my inner self. What happened after that I take full responsibility for, the mistakes I made were mine and I will have to answer for them. I have come to realize that my time with Musa was not meant to be a long one. Rather it was meant to be a short and intense communion that is meant to be cherished. I hope he still remembers me, not in the same way that I remember him since I can not in any way have meant the same for him as he meant for me. I can only wish he thinks fondly of our time together and that he can find gratification in that he helped me so much and was the cause of my religious awakening.

I haven't written much at all about what is going on right now, for the reason that almost nothing has happened. The food inventory is starting to run low so we will either have to go into town for more food again (might as well send the guy that already shaved his beard if you ask me) or make a move in order to try to find a place where we can hole up and hope we find something edible there. These two other guys just sit around and talk for the most part when they are not praying or reading the Quran. I just spend my time writing, pretty much all day as you can see by the amount that I have been putting down these last few days. My right hand is well conditioned by now and the cramps are a thing of the past. Thank God, الحمد لله. They were asking me yesterday about what I was writing. I answered that I was keeping a diary, that I just wanted to get some thoughts out and that I was also writing some poetry. They mostly shrugged at my response and didn't press me. Perhaps they just look at my writing as folly that has no value in this life or the next. They are wrong on that point if that is what they think. I'm trying to leave something behind to serve as a warning for anyone that might be thinking about walking in my destructive footsteps. If this doesn't reach anyone, then this sentence will certainly be futile. But much of what I'm writing I feel is therapeutic for me, so whether someone reads it or not, it still has value to me. As it serves as a way for me to examine my life and once again ponder what I have to be thankful for and what I need to beg God's forgiveness for before this is all over.

I left you at a crucial point in my story yesterday, one that I myself wonder about to this day. Today, I might be willing to accept that the way me and Musa got separated was the best possible scenario. Only because I'm convinced that Allah wants what is best for Musa and I am still hopeful that He wants the same for me. Sometimes goodbyes suck. They can be uncomfortable, awkward and very sad. On the flip side, it can be an opportunity to make future plans to reunite under new circumstances. The abrupt end can be good in the sense that it eliminates the sad, tearfilled farewell that some of us fall into when there is a strong emotional connection to the person we are saying goodbye to. I, like I explained perhaps too many times in order to emphasize it, had a very strong emotional connection to Musa for the reasons that I already laid out. I would most likely have been a sentimental wreck if me and him had a chance to sit down and say our farewells. So I will for the sake of my own sanity just concede that it happened the right way. Though at the time, my feelings about the situation would send my life into a tailspin that I would never recover from.

It was a regular day like most other days in the pen. Just the regular daily routines with nothing out of the ordinary taking place. We woke up and prayed the dawn prayer together, kicked it in the cell for a bit. Both of us went separate ways to read our book for that week. Someone in the group has picked Camus, The Fall. Little did I know at the time that the title would end up being topical. Me and Musa reconvened on the yard and did our workout routine, which was getting tougher each week as we were cranking it up. Afterward we had lunch together we went our separate ways again. I went to the library to read more of Camus and also work on my ever so slightly improving Arabic. I can't exactly remember how long I sat there, perhaps an hour or so. I needed some notes I had for my Arabic studies in our cell. I got stuck on some basic grammar problem and wanted to see what I had written down in my Arabic scrapbook. I made the walk back to the cell and sat down on the chair and started looking through my notepad, which led to (like it always seems to do with me) me looking through all loose papers and scrapbooks in the vicinity. I got lost in my many loose sheets and small notebooks as I forgot my original intent that made me go to the cell. The alarm brought me back to reality from the daze I was in as I was scanning all these random notes. When the alarm rang in that place, it *rang*. It was so loud that it was completely impossible to focus on anything else. Along with the eardrum shattering sirens, red light covered the walls as if we were in some type of disco nightclub. I kind of froze in my spot and when I realized what was going on I just kept on sitting in that same spot on the chair since there was no reason to make a move since I would be ushered right back into my cell in no time. When there was an alarm situation they closed off all areas. That meant that if you were in your cell, you would remain in your cell until the emergency was over. If you were in the library, then that would be the place you would have to wait in (not a bad place to wait if you ask me, as opposed to the showers for example). If you were in the yard you would have to stay in the yard. One would remain waiting like that until the situation was under control and they had isolated all those that were involved in the incident. There were only a few reasons for this ever happening. Inmates fighting with each other, inmates fighting with the COs, weapons or the like being found or perhaps some security breach that could lead to an escape attempt. It was impossible to know how long it would take the COs to get everything under control and let us continue with our daily routines. It could be anything from ten minutes to a couple of hours if things were really bad. In other words, one just had to be patient and wait. The thing about spending time in these institutions was that many of us became professional waiters (not of the restaurant variety). In this case I was in my cell, derailed from my studies. Since my purpose of going to the cell in the first place was to study, it felt like a good use of this lock down time would be to do just that. The sirens and the flashing red lights were turned off after about fifteen minutes or something like that. That only meant that the most acute part of the situation was manageable. How long it would take for them to sort everything and return to status quo was anybody's guess. We must have remained on lockdown for close to three hours that day. I remember thinking that we might end up missing dinner. We didn't, but it got delayed past its regular time. Like you know, when you are used to eating at a very specific time each day and you are hindered for whatever reason, it can affect your mood in strange ways. It didn't take long for the clock to move past our standard dinner time before all types of curses started to rain down from various tiers in our cellblock. Convicts started going crazy, hurling insults at the COs and talking about what they would do to their mothers and sisters. Yeah, it got rough in there sometimes. Eventually they started opening up our cells, doing it tier by tier, in order to not have the dining hall overflowed with hungry inmates who were extra edgy due to the delay of their suppers. Musa hadn't come back to our cell, obviously he couldn't because of the lockdown. He must have been isolated in whichever part of the facility he happened to be in when the alarm went off. I calmly just went out of the cell once they started opening the doors on our tier and I headed down to the dining hall together with a stream of other inmates who all seemed upset that their daily routine had been thrown off. I got in line and just waited to get my tray loaded with lusterless food. I figured that Musa would join whenever inmates in the section he happened to be in when the emergency happened were let out. I found a decent spot at one of the tables where a few guys I knew a little sat. I made some small talk but was mostly quiet as I gulped down the food. I was used to having every meal in the vicinity of Musa so eating without him felt strange. I kept scanning the dining area every now and then in order to see if he would pop up, but he never did. No big deal, I thought, he either came and ate before me or he was yet to be let out of wherever he happened to be in the prison and still waited to dine. I still didn't think about it as being strange, I just walked back to my cell. There wasn't all that much time before they would lock the doors anyway and I didn't really feel like hanging around in the recreation area and mingling with people, so I decided to just go back to our cell and chill out until they would lock us in for the evening.

When I came to my tier and started walking to my cell I was surprised to see several COs by the cell door. I walked over there to see what was going on, not sure that it was our cell they were standing by, it could just as well have been one of our neighbours. But sure enough, the closer I got I understood that it was our cell that they had some sort of issue with. They would do cell inspections on the regular, that was not a strange thing in itself. The hour was very strange though, as was the fact that they had brought a whole squad over there. Usually they would search cells in pairs, two COs deemed enough to handle that job. Something out of the ordinary was going on. They tried to make me keep walking in the tier when I reached my door, as if there was nothing there to see. I told them that this was my cell and asked why the hell they were turning it upside down at this hour. The only answer I got was: stand back. I tried not to lose my temper as I stood out there on the tier looking at them going through our stuff. Then they started asking me at random about different items: is this yours or your cellmate's? Whenever I said mine they threw that item on the floor and whenever I said his, they threw it in a big black trash bag. In other words they were taking away all of Musa's possessions. I stood there dumbfounded, not really getting what was going on. Why are they taking all his stuff away and where is Musa? All of a sudden I felt stupid that I had not connected the dots earlier, I should have suspected it as soon as I saw the COs gathered outside the cell door. The ordeal had to be connected to the emergency situation. Why would they otherwise come in at this strange hour and clean house. As I stood there realizing just that, I started hearing yelling from some of the other tiers. It sounded like angry complaints and I imagined that something similar to what was happening to me was also befalling others in this cell block. One of the COs held up Musa's Quran, no doubt his most prized possession. Yours or his, they asked me. I was stuck. First of all I was offended that the CO had picked up the Holy Book as if it was any regular piece of literature. Musa always handled that book with the greatests care and respect. On top of that, I was one hundred percent sure that the CO had not washed himself as is required before touching the Quran. I stood there confounded, not knowing how to react when the same guy yelled out, this time louder and with more anger in his voice:

"Yours or his?"

"Mine!"

I lied and he put the book on the desk and continued to inspect our belongings. I was second guessing my impulse afterwards as it might have meant that I had just taken something... not something, the most important thing from Musa. On the other hand, the alternative was to watch them throw it in the trash bag and only God knew where it would end up, if it would reach its actual owner or if it would have been thrown on some heap somewhere together with a bunch of garbage. I leaned back against the railing as they proceeded to inspect the cell meticulously, occasionally asking me to whom a certain item belonged. The others in our cellblock that were going through the same type of situation were not as patient and kept on unleashing insults at the COs that were looking through their cells. I sure wanted to as well but realized that this was a battle that I couldn't win, so going to war was not a feasible option. The one possible outcome was that they simply would get fed up with me for talking shit and throw me in the hole just to prove a point; who had the power and who didn't. The other possible outcome was that they would just become straight up irritated and pissed off at me without doing anything about it now, but holding that against me for the rest of my stay. Which would mean that I would have to take shit from them for the foreseeable future. Some COs would *never* forget an insult, and would remind you of it any chance that they got.

When they were finally done I entered the cell and sat down on the chair, looking at the damage they had done. They didn't bother to restore the cell to any type of order when they were done, it was left looking like what you might expect a cell looking like after things had been thrown around for more than thirty minutes. I started to put things in order while thinking about what the reason for all this could be. I also started realizing that Musa would not be coming back to this cell. If they had just thrown him in the hole for some reason they would have left all his belongings in its place. Instead they cleaned house, meaning that he would not return. I started preparing for the evening prayers, recognizing that I would be praying them by myself for the first time in months. As I looked around the cell it felt so empty with all his things removed and as I commenced my prayer the cell felt even emptier. I had a really hard time concentrating in my prayers that night as my thoughts about what had just happened kept spinning around in my head at a high velocity. I knew I was not going to be able to sleep right away so I layed in bed and just let my mind roam for a while. I was never one to listen much to the chatter on the tier at night, as me and Musa were always busy with some sort of activity. This night though, I was without a celly and listening to the conversations on the tier was the only thing that could take my mind off my own thoughts, which were moving in perpetual circles inside of my cranium.

As I started paying attention to what guys were talking about it became obvious that the topic of conversation was the incident that occured that same afternoon and affected the entire cell block in some way. I was content with just listening without chiming in or asking any questions. All types of theories floated around in the night air. As the night went on there seemed to be a consensus that developed that there had been some form of riot in the western side of the cell block on one of the top tiers, in one of the open areas that existed in that wing where inmates could gather. Some names were thrown around, people who were supposedly involved or even responsible for the ruckus. The names didn't mean anything as they were completely unknown to me. Then, after a short while it hit me. It was where the uncles used to hang out and also the place where they used to pray together. I started getting some type of idea of what might have happened and I gave up on trying to listen to the gabbling as I had reached the point where I was becoming less informed the more I heard. I went to sleep but had one of those nights filled with anxious sleep. You might know it. When you have something that is really troubling your mind. Yet you sleep, but you keep on waking up only to fall asleep again and the night passes in those types of spurts. Your conscious thoughts merging into your abstract dreams and the dream world infecting your mind for the periods when you are awake. I got up to pray the dawn prayer, not being sure if I had slept all night or laid there turning from side to side while cognizant the whole time.

I didn't even try to go back to sleep as I felt that it would be a waste of time to lay down and most likely just stare into the wall, the chance of falling asleep being slim. I sat on the floor and read the Quran for the remainder of the time until they opened the doors. As I tried my best to focus completely on the Arabic words it actually took my mind off the situation for the time being. When the doors finally opened it was as if reality slapped me in the face and reminded me of what had just happened. I left the world of the Divine word and slid into the cold reality of being deprived of my cellmate and best friend. My only mission that day was to find out what had happened and where Musa could possibly be. I had breakfast all by myself, trying to eavesdrop on a few conversations but nothing interesting caught my ear. So after I finished eating I started moving around in the open area where most of the inmates used to move around after breakfast, looking for someone that I could talk to in order to find out more. The thing with this prison, and I'm assuming the same holds true for many others, was that you couldn't just walk up to whomever and ask about whatever. There were some real decision makers in that place and if you wanted to talk to them you better go through the right channels and not just step right up to them, unless you were willing to deal with the consequences.

Fortunately for me I saw a guy from my tier that I had talked to a couple of times before and who was also acquainted with Musa. He also seemed to, based on the times I talked to him, always be aware of what was going on inside and outside the prison. The guy just gave the impression of being very well-rounded in his knowledge and knew a lot about almost everything. I caught Denard standing there leaning against a staircase talking to a scrawny Chinese guy who seemed very animated as he was trying to explain something to Denard. The Chinese guy was wearing the absolute smallest t-shirt that was available in the pen, his toothpick-thin arms moving in all directions simultaneously as he was making his case about something apparently very important to Denard. He had earrings in both ears and a hairdo that made him look like he belonged in some Beijing grunge band. The guy's name was Lewis, believe it or not. One of many, in my opinion, ill-chosen names adopted by young Chinese immigrants. Many called him Louie and the Latinos called him Louie Loco, which Lewis in prime out of touch immigrant fashion mistook for Louie Local, a name that many ended up preferring to call him by since everyone was in on the joke, except for Louie Local himself. I felt for him, honestly. He was this little Chinese guy who was in the States in order to go to school and started becoming way too interested in shrooms, acid and all types of pills. He got caught up in a raid that the police did at a rave in some forest where those rave kids thought they were safe. Lewis was out there selling all the stuff that he himself was using and got sentenced for possession with intent to sell. The guy was in his last year of college, probably financed by hard-working parents back home in China, and here he was doing time in the major league with all these veterans and rookies eager to prove they belonged. Fortunately for him he was a lovable character and many people in there looked out for him just because they had taken a liking to him. So you could mess with Lewis if you wanted to, but there might be repercussions coming your way from an unexpected source.

I looked Denard in the eyes as I stopped in my tracks while approaching him and Lewis. Denard gave me the sublelest of nods, undetectable to the uninitiated. I understood that it meant: just give me a second, let me finish here with Louie Local first. I gave them their space as I didn't want to intrude into their conversation. Denard was mostly nodding throughout Lewis' rant, which was getting longer and longer and more agitated. I thought for a second that the guy was about to start crying as he was showing a lot of emotion while expressing himself to Denard. A little too much emotion, many would say, since it was all displayed in public. Lewis got a pass though, just for being Louie Local. Finally Denard cut him off and told him:

"I got you. Alright? I'll take care of it, I promise. Don't beat yourself up."

Denard put his arm on Lewis' shoulder as a form of consolation.

"Thanks, man", was Lewis' reply.

He turned around and walked away, slightly shaking his head as if he couldn't quite understand his own plight. Denard gave me another nod, this one meaning: your turn. I stepped to him and before I could address him he greeted me with: "peace brother." I returned the greeting and I got straight to the point. Me and him had had plenty of short interactions over the months that we had been in the same cell block, but pretty much every time it had been in a group setting. Many times when I was together with Musa, as Denard and Musa seemed to be pretty close. Denard was probably the non-Muslim in prison that Musa talked to the most, excluding the guys in the book club. They had clicked on some level and since he knew that me and Musa were not just cellies, but rather more like brothers, I had an ally in Denard even though I didn't really know him personally. I asked him what he knew about what went down the previous day and if he knew what had happened to Musa and I told him how they had cleaned out our cell of all his belongings.

"Man!"

He really dragged the vowel out as if to indicate the severity of what he was about to tell me next.

"I've been told that he got caught up over there by where those older Muslims hang out. You know the spot?"

His voice was now low and sedated, for anyone to pick up on what was being said he would have to stand close enough for us to smell his breath. You could just tell that Denard was a pro at talking to all types of people in there about all types of things.

"You know, those Muslims have been under scrutiny for the longest time in here. You know how prison politics work, right? They have this "task force" in here that is monitoring all the gangs, interactions with each other, what the membership looks like, all that type of bullshit. I guess the security guys were over there in that area last afternoon, doing their searches and shit. And they came up on a few shanks and some other stuff and started talking about sending guys to the hole and writing reports. A couple of guys took issue with them being searched, saying that they are being unfairly targeted, that things are being planted and so on and so forth. It gets real heated between a few of the guards and two of the Muslims. Cooler heads *don't* prevail and one of the Muslims swings at the CO that is requesting back up to the area. All the COs jump on that guy which sets off a chain reaction and the COs get jumped as they are outnumbered and at that point, I'm assuming, can't go for their pepper spray and shit. The other COs arrived as backup as the alarm started going off. Were you on our tier at that time? Yeah, me too. We are too far away to hear what's going on in that part of the prison, right? So I just went in my cell and had no idea what was going down as it happened. Anyway, after the backup arrived, it basically turned into a brawl that got pretty violent. I mean, you know me a little, I don't really mess with those Muslims that Musa used to hang out with from time to time. I'm not a big fan of their politics and how they handle some stuff. But I'll tell you one thing bro, they don't take shit from anybody in here and that includes the people working here, you know? And *that* I can respect. Out of any group in here, that is who I want on my side if it really goes down. So I know that whatever they were subjected to, they weren't going to take it and move on. If they felt it was unjust in any way, they would fight it. Which is what they did I guess.

"Now, I don't know who did what and who didn't. I know who a few of those guys over there are and what they are about. But I haven't heard anything about who set it off and who got involved, who got hurt and so forth. I *do* know that Musa was over there though, that has been confirmed. What I also heard was that some of those guys went straight to the hole, butt ass naked. And that they are still there right now until they decide what to do with them. And that others have already been removed from the prison altogether. They have been sent to some other penitentiaries. Which ones, I have no clue. If they took your boy's stuff just like that though I would have to assume that he was one of the ones moved. They are trying to split them up since they see them as this gang constellation. I know Musa doesn't even get down with them like that but they have seen him hang out with those guys and spend time over there in that area and that is enough for him to be considered at the very least affiliated. Which is all it takes in here bro. They somehow connect you to the wrong people and you are guilty by association right away.

"They could still have moved him within the prison but I really doubt it. What I have been hearing was that they were moved to the hole and that the ones who weren't were sent away to other prisons in an attempt to break up their whole organization. My guess is we won't see Musa in here ever again. Sorry man, I know that was your boy. It's a cold world in here bro."

I was flabbergasted. I thanked Denard for enlightening me about the situation and just walked away without any deliberation. I just started walking without knowing where or even why. I walked stairs, I walked on tiers I had never even set my feet on before, aimlessly I was just moving along as my head would not stop spinning. Recess came and I kept walking outdoors, I walked the same route in the yard that me and Musa had walked day in and day out for months. I kept on trying to process what had happened but my mind could not find any rest. The closest thing I can compare how I felt to was being dumped and backstabbed by a girl you're in love with. This is a terrible analogy but it is the best one I can come up with. I write that since Musa had meant *so* much to me. He wasn't just a friend who I was close with. He was my teacher, my guide, my mentor. I truly believed and still believe that Allah sent him to me specifically… and then he was taken away, just like that, all of a sudden without warning. The big difference of course and where the analogy falters is that Musa did not leave me. Instead something else was responsible for our break up. Nonetheless, I was still heartbroken and was struggling to understand why it happened. I had taken his companionship for granted, until it was snatched away from me. If it was the hole he went to or any other place for that matter that I at least knew of, it would have been much easier to process. Then I would have at least known where he was and I could also reach out to him in one way or another. The way things unfolded I could just sit around and wait and hope that I would hear from him in some way.

I didn't eat lunch that day, my appetite was gone and there was no trace of it. Instead I spent time in my cell, trying to sort things out in my mind. The cell felt more and more empty by the minute after realizing that my cellie was not going to return. All his stuff was gone and had left an empty space that felt like a vacuum. The only thing remaining was his personal copy of the Quran. How fitting, I thought to myself. I was happy to have it and at the same time uneasy about having lied about it being mine. Wherever he was, his belongings would be forwarded to him and he would receive them sooner or later (according to the regulations at least). His most beloved possession would be missing though and I realized that he would probably take that pretty hard. I decided to not read my own copy any more and instead use Musa's old copy. If I knew one thing about him it was that he wanted the Quran to be *read*, not to be a mere decoration.

I forced myself to eat some dinner that day even though I would have prefered not to. The problem was that if I didn't I would probably regret it by night time when I lay in my cell staring at stale cookies and noodle packages. I sat by myself and ate that day, not in the mood for interaction with anyone. A few guys said hi as they walked by and I returned their greetings, other than that I didn't have any communication with anyone. I layed in my bed that night, still trying to make sense of what had happened and why. He was the one that told me that there was no such thing as "wrong place, wrong time". So I couldn't just say that that is what happened to him. According to him, and also to my newfound belief, there had to be a purpose behind even this occurrence. Whatever it was, I couldn't discern it. I couldn't submit to this fate that I had been handed, which I now understand was proof of the weakness of my faith (the student was still light years behind his teacher). So instead of submitting I got angry, it was the natural outlet for me when things got tough. When my mother was harassed, I got angry. When me and my brother felt like we were treated unfairly, we got angry. When our father died, I felt anger. Probably a result of not having a deeper perspective on why things might happen to us, Musa had explained that to me many times. Anger didn't solve any problems, but it could create a plethora of new ones. Often setting off a negative cycle that would be hard to escape. Some of this I understood at that time but not profoundly. Rather, it was theoretical and when it really hit the fan, like it did when Musa disappeared, I reverted to my old self and let anger be my way of dealing with the frustration.

My desk took a pounding that night, at the expense of my poor knuckles. My neighbour asked me if I was entering the cuckoo's nest. Not a strange occurrence in that environment. I tried to gather myself by washing vigorously and then performing my evening prayers. It helped for a little while. More accurately, it helped in the very moment when I was praying. After that I regressed to a state of anger and frustration. I fell asleep mad that night and woke up mad. I remained mad for the entire day after waking up. Then the next day I met someone that would explain that my anger was justified and that there was a way out of it. A way I had never thought of before and which led me to the predicament I'm in right now.

October 21st

It's been two weeks now since I started writing. I'm scared I might run out of paper. Thankfully I learned how to write *really* small. Musa was the one who put me on to that. It's a good skill to have in prison since a lot of communication between inmates is written and the smaller the letters, the smaller the paper you can use. Which obviously is harder to detect and easier to flush. So hopefully I should be alright going forward as far as writing material is concerned. How much time I have is in God's control. We have decided that we are making another move tomorrow. Predawn we will try to get to our next location where we can bunker up. It is very dangerous to move at any time right now. The darkness presents both an advantage and a challenge. The advantage is that if you are quiet enough and experienced in night travel, you can move undetected. The big challenge is that if you are in an area that your opponent knows better than you, then you are at a major disadvantage. In other words, travelling by night like this will be a gamble. One worth taking though since the three of us are in agreement that it would be much riskier to try to move in the daylight hours. We are at the point where we have no choice. It's either find a new spot or head back into town to get more food supplies. We will have to find new lodging sooner or later anyway so we might as well change locations this upcoming night. Today's nutritional intake will consist of less than a handful of raisins, a few nuts and water from the faucet which might or might not contain parasites. I need to get back to my story though if I'm going to have any chance of finishing it.

It was two days after Musa's sudden disappearance and I was sitting in my bed doing nothing in particular. I remember that I had prayed the noon prayer not long ago and that I was sitting there still trying to figure out the situation after having been informed by Denard what the most likely scenario had been that led to Musa's expulsion. No new information had come to me since I spoke to Denard and thinking about the situation had reached the point of a dead end, still it was impossible for me to let it go. The wounds were still too fresh and the pain from them fueled my anger constantly and since I didn't really have an outlet for my ever growing rage it made the madness fester like an infected wound. My thoughts had taken me far away from the cell I was sitting in but I was abruptly pulled back into the present by the cacophonic sound of a baton being dragged against the bars of the cell. Sometimes the COs would do this to catch your attention when they felt like you were not worth a courteous "excuse me". I looked up towards my cell door and saw two COs standing there. I just gave them a look that could only mean: what do you want? One of them said:

"Your new celly."

A guy appeared in the doorway looking me straight in the eyes. The two COs walked away, their duty having been fulfilled. The new guy looked away from my face as his eyes scanned the room. I noticed that his vision got fixed on two items as he was checking out his new living accomodation. The Quran that was laying open on the desk and the prayer rug that was still on the floor. His stare returned to my eyes and he greeted me with: salam alaykum. I returned his greetings and told him to take a seat. He hesitated for a short while before settling down on the wooden chair by the desk while simultaneously putting down a plastic bag with his belongings on the floor. I extended my hand and told him my name, he took it and presented himself as Taymour. I had a hard time figuring out where this guy could be from. He was kind of round with thick, black hair that almost reached his shoulders and a beard to match. His face looked almost Asian, I would probably have guessed Mongolian even though I would feel rather certain that the guess would be wrong. His eyes had a weird darkness to them that is hard to explain. They had this depth to them, but not in a good way. His face was pockmarked and there was something edgy about his energy.

We sat down and talked for a while. It turned out that he was basically completely new in this place so I decided to show him around a little bit while making some conversation. He told me he was Uzbek, meaning from Uzbekistan. It was the first time I had ever met anyone from there and probably about the third time that I had even heard about the country. He had only been in the States for about three years but spoke English very well, having lived in the UK prior to coming over. His English was very good in the grammatical sense, but he had a very strong accent that he would probably carry around for the rest of his life. He had a little less than a year that he had to do in this prison. It could have been way more but the charges didn't really stick the way the prosecutor was hoping for, but he *did* get caught with explosives. Thankfully for Taymour, his lawyer got him a very good sentence through some very clever juridical maneuverings. Not easy in the US post 9/11, with a Muslim client and explosives involved. I didn't ask about his case. Those were the unwritten rules in this place. If asked, you had to say what you were in there for but after that it was considered bad etiquette to probe into someone's past crime history like that. Here he was though, my new Muslim roomate. I tried to just give him the basics when it came to the routines in prison, the do's and don'ts, who you could talk to and who you shouldn't. He didn't say much, instead he was taking everything in. He seemed contemplative and at times distant in his mind. A few times I had to ask myself if this guy was even listening to me.

When we got back to the cell later he insisted on leading the prayer. I wasn't against that since I still felt like a novice, but I was a little taken aback by his insistence on doing it. It gave me the sense that he might have apprehensions about praying together if I was the one leading the prayer. I could tell that he knew what he was doing though. He knew his stuff and he seemed to handle Arabic even better than Musa did. It didn't take many conversations before he started telling me how knowledgeable he was about Islam and how much he had studied. He started dropping names left and right of his teachers, who were all totally unknown to me. It became obvious that he was making it a point to show that he knew more than me. Something that I would happily concede since I was still so new in the faith. I didn't have any delusions about being better or more learned or pious than the next brother, on the contrary. He had an edge to his voice also, when he spoke he came off as kind of aggressive. Even when talking about mundane things there was like an underlying aggression in his tone. It was a little strange to me and it was in sharp contrast to Musa who was not mellow at all when speaking, but rather he was balanced and calculated. Musa seemed like the kind of guy you couldn't easily rattle in a conversation. While Taymour came off as the opposite, he could get riled up rather fast when discussing something.

I was pleased to have a new cellmate though. A few extra

days alone wouldn't have been the worst thing in the world but it was most likely for the best that he showed up when he did. My thoughts were still spinning when he appeared and my anger was simmering, if not boiling. So having been left to myself for a longer period of time would probably have made me nutty since I didn't really know how to channel my thoughts and deal with my anger about what had just happened. On top of that, my new celly was a Muslim. What were the odds of that happening? Two Muslim cellmates in a row. Not only that, a Muslim cellmate that actually practiced his religion. I saw it as some sort of sign that Taymour showed up when I had just been deprived of my best friend. A friend who had taught me how to pray, how to read the Quran, how to fast. He had really shown me the ropes. Then, right after he disappears, I get a new cellmate that can teach me as well. So it was almost as if my religious education didn't skip a beat. That could only be from God since I know how rare it is to get *one* person in your life that provides exactly what you need at the right time. Now I had received two in a row with basically no gap in between. It just could not have been a coincidence. I didn't expect Taymour to take Musa's place in any real sense since that would be impossible in my world, considering that Musa was the one that really opened up my heart for the love of Islam. That could never be duplicated. What he could provide me with though, was more teaching, starting more or less from the point where me and Musa had left off. Little did I know that Taymour would provide me with much more than that. He would open up my eyes to a whole new world view and provide a direction for me in life that had hitherto been completely nonexistent. He would convince me of how

I could set everything right and fulfill my highest purpose in this God-given life, but I'm getting way ahead of myself. It would take a couple of months before I was ready to jump in head first to the mission proposed by Taymour. Before I reached that point he shrewdly and skillfully explained my predicament to me and gave me the reasons for why they existed. He was clever enough to not tell me about the solution right away. Instead, he methodically talked to me and convinced me *how* and *why* I had reached the situation that I found myself in. Once again, I'm jumping the gun, so please excuse me. Let me take you back to when Taymour's lessons truly started. It was on our third day together in the evening as we were sitting in our cell after they had locked the doors for the evening.

He looked at my desk and noticed that I had two different copies of the Quran laying there. He hadn't touched any one of them up to that point. The guy liked to sit on the prayer rug and recite from memory it seemed like. During the first couple of days he never once asked if he could borrow my Quran. That evening though, he asked to look at them. I handed him my own first, which he looked through and then handed back to me. After that I gave him Musa's copy, which was the one that I used to read after Musa's disappearance. He looked through that one also while lifting one of his eyebrows as if expressing extra interest. He asked me why I had two of them. Instead of answering the question I asked him if he would like to have one of the two copies. He gladly accepted and repeated the question which I had just avoided answering. I just told him that I had a cellmate right before him that got transferred and that his Quran was left behind.

"What happened to him?", Taymour asked me.

I wasn't really sure what to reply since I wasn't sure that I was ready to talk about it, much less to someone who was basically a complete stranger. Though the fact that Taymour was a Muslim and that we had already prayed together had given me a level of trust in him that I wouldn't otherwise have with someone that I had met a couple of days ago. Yet, I wasn't sure that I was ready to open up about it. There was a strong chance that I would get emotional when talking about it and that would make me feel exposed in front of someone that I had just met and would be forced to live with. That form of emotional transparency could easily be perceived as weakness in prison and if there was one thing you did not want to be seen as, it was just that, weak. He must have noticed my hesitation while he waited for my response. It must have shown on my face that I was really weighing the pros and cons of telling him the story.

"Are you scared of telling me, brother?"

He asked with a wicked smile on his face that was impossible to interpret. I thought that it could probably be therapeutic to tell him, to let it out, emotions be damned. Also, by not telling him and keeping it a secret, or coming up with some peculiar lie, he might think that *I* was the reason for my cellmate being moved. Which would lead to an environment filled with suspicion, not the best for cohabitation.

So I decided to lay it all out. I figured, if I'm going to live with this guy I might as well be honest. It would be wrong to lie and on top of that, if I did and he later found out the true version of the event from others, it would be a disaster for my reputation. So I started from the beginning by telling him about how me and Musa met and got to know each other, how our friendship grew and got stronger with time until it was a bond that felt stronger than blood ties. I didn't go into all the details of course, it would have made for too long of a story, but I gave him enough for him to understand why our bond had become so strong. I also explained how Musa had introduced me to Islam and how important he had been to my interest and also level of commitment in the faith. I had no problems admitting that I still considered myself a novice and that my level of knowledge was rudimentary at best. Taymour sat there listening and seemed to be really locked in and interested. He sat on the chair, leaning forward with his elbows on his knees while I sat on the bed. An expression of concern mixed with curiosity was apparent on his countenance. His interest seemed to intensify as my story moved along and finally climaxed with the incident that led to Musa being removed from my cell and placed God knows where. Taymour really perked up when I told him about the uncles and how Musa used to hang out with them on occasions. I also told him some of the things Denard had shared with me about how the prison administration had labeled them a gang and kept their eye on them for the longest. Hearing these things made Taymour move around in his seat, hardly being able to contain himself, as if I was spilling government secrets or something like that, that he had been dying to hear for a long time. He was nodding in agreement as I was filling out the picture and got to the point where he was shaking his head in agreement (if you can picture that) when I told him about the alleged incident that happened on that now notorious afternoon a few days ago.

I almost surprised myself by how matter-of-factly I could deliver all the information. My emotions didn't really get in the way of telling it like it truly was and I also didn't expose myself as the emotional wreck that I felt that I was on the inside (thank God!). It also felt great in a sense to let it all out. These had been the thoughts that had been spinning around inside me ad nauseum for the last few days. I think it also helped a lot to have a listener that seemed genuinely interested in what I had to share. It was as if Taymour's interest in my story kept peaking as the story moved along. He became more locked in with every sentence that I uttered and everything else in the world was losing significance at the same rate as his interest was increasing. When I was done with the story, which culminated with the sudden disappearance of Musa and my feelings of anger that had accompanied it, Taymour leaned back in the chair and looked at the ceiling while presumably taking it all in. He seemed to ponder all that I had said for a rather long moment of silence before going into a long soliloquy that would be the first chapter of my new indoctrination. I don't remember it exactly verbatim, which would be hard since it was rather long and it happened a little over a year ago, but if you allow me to paraphrase just a little bit I can give you a very honest rendition.

"I understand and I'm not surprised. That's how it always goes for us. You see, our enemies are everywhere, constantly trying to make our project falter. This would never have happened to you or your friend if you weren't Muslims. You have to understand that this is what our enemies want, to degrade us and make us feel downtrodden. Anytime they see us becoming stronger in any type of way they will try to break us, using any method that they can. You see, you just told me that they had been monitoring those older Muslims in here. And I agree with you, they were looking for the smallest infraction. Then they all got sent away, your cellmate included, even though he really didn't have anything to do with them. Trust me, they would have sent you far away too if you happened to be there that day.

"Now, let me ask you something. You have been here for a pretty long while, compared to me at least who just got here. I know the answer to this question before even asking you but I will ask you anyway. Have you seen any other "gang" in here getting treated like that? Humiliated and then broken up, deported?"

This guy had a point, I hadn't seen anyone else in here getting that type of treatment. Not the whites, not the Salvadorans, not the Puerto Ricans. It was only us Muslims who got handled in that way. Just like I had his attention while telling him about Musa's vanishing, he had mine, totally undivided, as he was laying out the case for why it was this way.

"Brother, this is not just happening here. And it's not just happening everywhere in this country. It is happening all over the *world*. Our enemies are humiliating us and they won't stop until we strike back. Think back on your life, how much negativity have you endured just because you are Muslim?"

The question hung in the air like a foul odor.

My mind started moving backwards to my childhood days. Yes, my mother being harassed. My sister getting teased. Me and my brother getting made fun of in school. My father's ailment, which I'm convinced was an indirect effect of what the family as a whole was going through. How they made fun of us and our religion in the group homes. How the workers at juvy provoked us just because of our religion. Taymour was right. My entire life it had always been present in one way or another. We obviously had enemies that wanted to hurt us, emotionally and/or physically. There was no doubt about that.

"There is a way out of this though, and only one way. We have to fight back and we have to fight back hard. As long as we don't do that they will never take us seriously. Fire has to be fought with fire. You understand?"

I was tripping, was he talking about setting off another quasi-riot in here?

"No, not in here brother. We can't win in here. They outnumber us and they have all the resources. It's a losing fight if we fight in here. We are within their system and we can never win in their system. We might be able to hurt them, but we can't win in their home. We have to start by fighting them in *our* home, within *our* system."

I didn't exactly get what he was talking about, I have to admit that some of the things he seemed to be indicating went over my head. Which was not unusual when it came to religious discussions, considering my low level of knowledge. Even though I did not get exactly what Taymour was getting at, it still hit my soul in a certain way since I could relate to all of it. His ideas were not alien, on the contrary I could recognize what he was talking about. It appealed to me since I knew that he didn't know about my past, yet he was spot-on in what he was describing. He sounded a little aggressive as he was pontificating, but perhaps aggression was what was needed to stop this form of oppression.

"Think about it brother, when did being a pacifist ever solve any problems? That Ghandi shit doesn't work brother, we are Muslim. Our Prophet was a warrior, akhi. He was brave, he fought his enemies and so did his companions. We are not meant to sit at home and take this type of abuse, Allah wants us to fight back. You know what happens when we sit back and watch them treat us like this without putting up a fight? They keep on doing it and it gets worse and worse. The only way to stop them is to play their game. They fight us, we fight back. They hit us, we hit back, *harder*. Do you get what I'm telling you?"

Yes, I did. His point was clear. His agitation was growing as his monologue became longer. I had never really heard anyone talk in this way before, but I had to admit that he was making some sense. He seemed to be about it, so to speak. He appeared to be someone that was actually ready to do something about this messed up situation. The more I started thinking about how mad I was about them taking Musa away and the more I thought about all the wrongs that my family had gone through, the angrier I got and the more sensible his point of view became.

Musa had always been very calm for the most part, he was collected and thoughtful, calculated you might say. I appreciated that a lot about him. The things that Taymour was now opening up my eyes to made me think that there might be a time when the calm and mellow approach was not the ideal one. Had calmness and coolness stopped my mother from being spat on? Had it parried any insults thrown our way? Had it averted looks in the form of darts aimed with precision at our souls? No, no and no. Another methodology might have helped though and Taymour had just planted that seed in me. This injustice that these brothers had just been a victim of, could it be avoided in the future by using meek means? I started to understand that it wouldn't. Perhaps Taymour was on to something.

We kept talking, deep into the night. He seemed to have it figured out. The way he was presenting his arguments it was obvious that they weren't haphazard. They were really thoroughly planned. It wasn't just a spontaneous reaction to what I had just told him, rather it was a premeditated response that he had prepared for the day it would come in handy.

As the days moved on we kept talking and he kept on convincing me that his viewpoints about how to solve conflicts and take Muslims out of their quandaries were the right ones. We kept on praying together more or less following the same schedule that me and Musa had followed. Taymour didn't mix at all with the other inmates, that was one of the big differences between him and Musa. Musa had others that he was at least semi-close to and didn't mind mingling with prisoners that he did not have any real affiliation to. Taymour on the other hand shunned company if it wasn't mine. He would keep to himself in the general area inside the prison and in the yard he would walk around by himself if I didn't join him or he would just find a spot in the sunshine and post up. I kept on doing my workout routine by myself and kept the few acquaintances that I had, though I spent less and less time with them and more with Taymour, under the spell of his slick rhetoric. I kept going to the book club (something which Taymour had absolutely no understanding of) and kept reading my books in the cell (which Taymour glanced at as if they were toxic), but my time and attention was steadily shifting to Taymour and this new world that he had brought me.

The thing that made me very attracted to his message was twofold. Firstly, his message was always "Islamic-centric". There were no parts of his arguments that were not connected to the Quran or the sayings of the Prophet (صلى الله عليه و سلم). He wasn't grabbing things out of thin air, but rather, all of it seemed to be coming directly from our religion. Not to say that Musa's viewpoints were not, but I could not see the correlation all the time. When I started thinking back, a lot of Musa's rhetoric might as well have been philosophy. Nothing wrong with that you might say. Well, it was according to Taymour. In his mind, *everything* had to come directly from Islam, or else it was worthless. In my mind at that time, that type of reasoning made sense. If Islam is the truth, which it is, others truths must be derived from it (please forgive the logic I was using back then, I don't hold the same position today.

Now I see it as much more nuanced, but this is not a philosophical dissertation, so I will spare you). Mind you, the thing that made Taymour's arguments so convincing to me was that he always tried (and in my mind at that time, succeeded) to base every religious and ideological standpoint that he took, on the Quran. He would recite the verses in Arabic and then tell me what they meant in English. Me, still being a low-level beginner in classical Arabic had no choice but to trust this "expert's" rendition of the translation. Because of that, his stance always became very authoritative in my eyes. Secondly, this guy was all about solutions. He saw a problem; the unjust treatment and oppression of Muslims all over the world at the hands of the unbelievers. Then he had a solution; fight this evil, satanic opponent until they are all gone and *we* can rule according to God's just laws. If you believe in God and His message to mankind, why wouldn't you want to live in a system that is based directly on God's commandments?

So how were we to go about this transformation of the world order and achieve this utopia on planet earth? He had an answer for this too. Much like Musa, Taymour always had answers, never lacking in that department. Now I wish I was only exposed to the former's answers and not the latter's, but that was the path I was meant to walk. Now, here I am. I will get to the rest of Taymour's plan and how he laid it out, but I will have to excuse myself as sleep is starting to overpower me and I don't want to write that part while not being sharp in my mind. Since it is perhaps the most important part of this message that I will leave behind, as it explains how I could fall for his trick (Taymour's or Satan's, you pick. If you answer: both, it is a valid answer). So let me get back at you tomorrow when (and off course if) we get to our new resting place. Until then…

Salam
A

October 22nd

—————

We made it to our new house. No moving-in party though. The sun just exposed itself fully in the east and daylight is present after a long pitch-black night. Two of us slept a few hours last night as the third guy kept watch. He woke us both up at the agreed-upon hour and we set out to look for this new place that we could maintain in for some time before continuing our quest to God knows where. It was pitch black as we moved through a terrain that was basically desert. It was *cold* last night, and still kind of is, but the morning sun usually annihilates the night cold swiftly upon its arrival. I'll tell you, there is no cold like desert cold, at least not in my opinion. I have experienced my fair share of North American East coast winters, and yes, they can be rough. Desert cold is different though, it penetrates your skin and gets inside your bones. Fortunately the adrenaline rush of the night travel and its uncertainties numbed me to the low temperature and chilling wind. The guy who had stayed up all night said he had the route figured out and knew how to orient himself based on where the sun set and how the stars lined up in the night sky. It might as well have been bullshit on his behalf but we didn't really have any objection since neither one of us knew where we were going. It was all guesswork. The different directions did not mean much, they were all assumptions based mostly on hope and prayers.

All we could hope for was to find a place to rest at without running into enemies. We managed both and now we are stationed in this small mud house that amazingly enough has running water. There are a few other houses in close proximity which we also checked out. They all seemed abandoned but must have been inhabited not long ago at all since we found bread in one of them that is still edible, as well as dates that we can probably live on for a few days. It's hard to tell what else is surrounding this area since we haven't dared to venture out after the light of dawn colored the landscape we dwell in. Both my comrades are out right now, out as in, in deep unconscious sleep. We prayed the dawn prayer together in this shelter as soon as the light was visible in the east and then they both knocked out directly afterwards. I was too high on adrenaline to relax and try to fall asleep. Instead I stayed by the window, reading the Quran for a little bit, the dawn light acting as my lamp. Then I rested a little, but I was still too riled up to be able to pass out. So I picked up pen and notebook and started writing. I will keep writing until I feel tranquil enough to enter the dream world, and when I wake up I will proceed.

The weeks kept moving along and my interest in Taymour's ideas were increasing steadily. He impressed me so much with his knowledge about Islam. He gave the appearance of a scholar as he cited Quranic verses and prophetic hadiths in Arabic from memory in his sermons with an audience of one. He was making it clear that the only solution to the worldwide Muslim struggle was to take up a military battle and fight the enemy. I dared not call him out directly, so in a roundabout way I asked him why we didn't do anything in here. I felt that I had just been oppressed myself when Musa was removed, and even more so, Musa and the uncles had been oppressed when they received that unfair treatment. We had injustices and a struggle to pick up right here if we wanted to. He always reiterated the response he gave me when I had raised the query in the very beginning of our acquaintance. The struggle is not here, we can't win here, *yet*. The real struggle right now is elsewhere, in the Middle East. To be exact, in Syria and in Iraq. To join that struggle and establish a neo-caliphate, based on the caliphate of the old glory days of Islam, *that* should be our only focus. *That* was the duty of *every* Muslim, and those who forsake this obligation and noble cause are our enemies just as much as the unbelievers are our enemies.

He was clever enough to always bring up the discrimination and maltreatment that me and my family had faced, no matter where in the country we had lived. Hearing this it obviously fueled my anger and resentment towards the invisible other that was always present, ready to dole out more oppression and suffering. I had opened up to him and told him all these personal stories and Taymour was savvy enough to use those memories to his advantage while recruiting me to his cause. The more I started to get attached to his preaching, the more I started to abhor anything that wasn't islamic. It was all or nothing with this guy. Either it was Islam or it was falsehood and delusion. The one thing I knew for sure was that the way I had lived my life so far and how I had related to all the challenges we had faced as Muslims, me and my family, hadn't led to any form of improvement in our condition.

Slowly I started to distance myself from all the non-Muslims in the prison. Not that I was close to them before, but occasionally I would hang out with those guys. Some of the guys from the book club for example, I wasn't opposed to taking a walk with one of them in the yard or discussing something with another one of them by the chess tables, or just shooting the breeze with Louie Local just for the fun of it. I scaled back, or rather, basically eliminated all of that. There were a few other Muslims in our cell block, I had never really socialized much with them before. The only reason was that, outside of Islam, I really didn't have much in common with them. Different ages, different backgrounds, grew up in different cultures. Now, all of a sudden, it struck me that they might be valuable allies in this struggle that Taymour had introduced me to. He shot it down right away when I brought my idea to his attention.

"Trust me, it will be a waste of time. I know those guys, I already talked to them and they don't see the truth in this struggle. They are blind to it and may Allah make them blind on Judgement Day. They will disassociate themselves from you completely if you even bring up the topic. And let me tell you, those people are the *worst*. They are even worse than these *kuffar*, these disbelievers. Why? Because they portray themselves as Muslim while truly being hypocrates. Some of them even pray, they claim to give charity. But when you mention to them the obligation of defending the Muslim land

and Islam's honour, they scoff at you and look down on you. You mention that our women are being raped and our children are made orphans, *right now*, even *today* it is happening. And they turn their back to you. At least our enemies tell us that they hate us, or if they don't tell us they show us by their actions. These hypocrites pretend to be with us but in reality they side with the *kuffar*. So they threaten us from within. Watch out for those people, they will corrupt you if they get the chance. My advice is to stay away from them completely."

I could see his point. What good were our prayers, our fasting, our religious studies if our brothers and sisters were suffering at different places at this very moment, while we are content with praying at home. If we are content with just praying and fasting, going to the mosque and having a job that pays and a nice little family to keep us company, far away from all the wars. What does that make us in the eyes of God? The more I thought about it (and heard about it, since Taymour would never shut up) the more convinced I felt that I had to make an impact. There seemed to be an opportunity for me to actually make a change in this world, to make it a better place for those who truly believed in Allah and His Messenger, صلى الله عليه وسلم. For the very first time I started getting convinced that there was a purpose for me in this life. I mean, Musa had explained our purpose to me clearly. God created us to worship Him and get to know Him. That sounded great, but it didn't give me any instructions as far as what I should be doing with the twenty four hours that I have been given each and every day. Sure, I can use it to worship God, that goes without saying. The rest of the time though? What should I do then? That is where Taymour's vision came into play. His plan included a purpose for the individual that was willing to see it. I could fulfill my obligations towards Allah by worshipping Him through rites *as well* as through establishing the caliphate that would bring Islam its glory of yesteryear and provide a safe haven for the believers and an end to the injustices.

It seemed like a win-win proposition, worshiping the Creator and making the world a better place all at once. At the same time, what was there for me to do in this place anyway? This country had provided me with nothing but misery and hard times, ditto for my family and all the other Muslims I knew. Finally someone seemed to have a solution and a plan to bring the solution into effect. I'll tell you what really made his plan, his ideas and his vision so compelling and convincing. It was that it did not sound like *his* plan, it was God's plan. This is what God wanted us believers to do. How so?, you might ask. Taymour always quoted the Quran and the prophetic hadith while preaching. He was extremely skillful in using the appropriate verses and prophetic sayings and inserting them in the proper places of his oration. It always had the effect of amplifying the point he was trying to make. To make it sound even more authoritative, he read the verses and the sayings in what sounded to me like flawless Arabic, then he would translate them into English. Adding to the level of my astonishment at his verbosity was the fact that this guy was not even Arab, yet seemed to master the language better than my parents.

He talked about leaving this morally desolate country and moving to the caliphate, the Islamic state. The model society, built on the precedence set by the Prophet Muhammad. Emigrating there was an obligation for every able Muslim male and female. He emphasized the importance of fighting the enemy actively in order to weaken them and at the same time strengthening the caliphate so that it could expand. The takeover of the entire world was the goal. Lofty you might think, for a band of men with control over a very limited territory in the Middle East. It had been prophesied though, and those blessed words would come true, one way or another. We might as well be the ones setting that prophecy in motion in order to get a share of the enormous reward that is promised to those that established God's law on the earth and strive militarily in His path.

When talking about how we should treat enemies who oppose us he would drop the majestic quotation in Arabic and follow it up with his impromptu translation. "Kill the idolaters wherever you find them, and take them captive and besiege them and wait for them in every ambush…"

He would try to boost courage by reciting something like: "Fight against them so that Allah will punish them by your hands and humiliate them and give you victory over them…"

Taymour was clever enough in his sermons to be able to spin it in such a way that our opponents were not just those who were actively fighting the holy state over there in Syria and Iraq. No, rather our enemies included many other "fellow Muslims". He would quote something along the lines of: "Fight those who don't believe in Allah and the Last Day, and don't hold that forbidden which hath been forbidden by Allah

and His Messenger, nor acknowledge the religion of Truth…"
What was this forbidden thing he was implying? Of course
he meant neglecting the obligation to help our poor brothers
and sisters in need. It was totally forbidden to forsake them
and their safety and obviously also forbidden to disown the
islamic state. As for those that did not deem this type of neglect and lack of support for our siblings in Islam as forbidden, they were also our enemies, *even* if they called themselves Muslims. Again, he reiterated, our biggest enemies exist
within our own ranks.

When trying to motivate and/or strike fear in me he
would use something like the following. "You who believe!
What is the matter with you, that, when you are asked to go
forth in the cause of Allah, you cling heavily to the earth? Do
you prefer the life of this world to the Hereafter? But little is
the comfort of this life, as compared with the Hereafter. Unless you go forth, He will punish you with a grievous penalty,
and put others in your place." I became terrified when hearing these types of verses recited. His delivery of his message
was strong enough in itself. Then, when the Quranic verses
were added to emphasize his points, the power of the arguments became irresistible.

It wasn't all fear-mongering though, he would also add
positive motivation by citing something such as: "Allah hath
purchased of the believers their persons and their goods; for
them in return is the Garden: they fight in His cause, and slay
and are slain: a promise binding on Him in truth…" If that
promise was not enough, he would magnify the glory that
awaited by enumerating all the blessings we would find once
we reached this new state of ours that our brothers had esta-

blished. A just society with welfare that would make Scandinavia blush. Oilfields that would guarantee that the state prospered financially for the foreseeable future. Many women who were already living there and even more who were anxiously waiting for their opportunity to undertake the emigration, all ready to marry a warrior who fought for the cause. None of them would dare to object in the slightest if you took a second wife, or a third, or a… Money was not a problem over there. We would be well-paid as soldiers fighting for the state. Especially since we were coming from a land far away. Those soldiers that were true migrants and not just joining from one of the adjacent territories, got paid double the amount of the local soldiers. That's because we had made a much bigger sacrifice by moving all the way over there, leaving our families and our comfortable lifestyles behind in order to dedicate our lives to the state. Luxuries were promised as an earthy reward for the striving, and only Allah knew what was in store for us in the hereafter.

Taymour said that he knew several brothers from the UK that had left that hub of satanism in order to join the caliphate. He also claimed to have met brothers here in America that had made the same journey, right before he was locked up. He was still in touch with important decision makers. As soon as he was let out of this prison, he would make his own emigration. It was only a matter of time for him, his mind was made up. He warned me about listening to others about this matter and cautioned me to even mention it to other Muslims. Never forget, he said one day, and cited the verse: "Therefore listen not to the unbelievers, but strive against them with the utmost violence." Always aware of reminding me that included in this category of unbelievers were the Muslims who were against this obligatory cause. They were one and the same as the enemy and we should be just as aware of their machinations as we are of the plotting of the unbelievers.

He constantly brought up the topic of hijra, migration for the sake of God. He would cite prophetic sayings about hijra as well as enumerate many Quranic verses which praised the migrants who were held in a very high esteem by God. This brought me back in time a little as I remembered that Musa had told me about this hijra from Mecca to Medina by the Prophet Muhammad and his companions. It was a seminal moment in the history of Islam and one of the major reasons why the religion was able to prosper. The believers left what was at that time the pagan city of Mecca for the monotheistic haven of Medina. That is where the Muslims could set up their state and achieve independence and self governance. So when I was thinking back on what Musa had told me about that part of the Prophet's biography, it struck me how much it resonated with Taymour's grand plan of leaving heathen America for the promised caliphate in Syria.

Some of it sounded harsh to me, it did. That harshness was easy for me to overlook though due to the high level of conviction I had experienced after my many talks with Taymour. What I perceived as harshness, I instead blamed on my own flaws. I was not strong enough in my faith and my knowledge had not become deeply rooted enough for me to be able to accept God's message the way it was meant to be understood. What are personal preferences compared to the will of God? Not worth much, I reckoned. That these verses and hadiths which he quoted were out of context and not at all connected to the type of battle and migration that Taymour was talking about, did not cross my mind at that point. It all seemed not only relevant, but also directly related to the issues he was convincing me about. That these Quranic verses and prophetic sayings were mentioning specific situations in specific places and in specific times, without being intended to be universalized did not ever dawn on me. Not at that time at least, not as I was travelling to this place I'm at now and neither when I touched down and became an active member of this so-called caliphate.

That realization only came to me later, or rather recently, at a time when it's too late for intents of worldly purposes. In the moment, when I was hearing those verses recited and then translated, it was as if God was speaking to me indirectly through Taymour. All this talk about our enemies just made too much sense when I thought about my (at that time) current situation and also as I thought about my and my family's past. It wasn't just a case of it sounding good and striking a chord with me, the thing that really made me a follower of this man's ideology was that he had a solution. A pathway that would lead to a better world, in which I could be an active member making a difference and gaining rewards for the next-coming life. It was a deal that sounded too good to be true. Turns out, it wasn't true, but my naivete did not allow me to see that at that point in time. The plan provided a purpose for someone that had for most his life lived without one. It provided a clear direction and a clear role for me to play in this project to restore Islam's dignity. It also gave me a great opportunity to leave this oppressive and unjust country and relocate to a place that seemed better than any type of society you could imagine.

The sense of a moral obligation to undertake this mission grew stronger and stronger the more time I spent with Taymour, listening to his sermons and praying together with him. All the questions and hypothetical objections were met with razor-sharp answers, the likes of which I would not dare to rebut. Taymour's own conviction in combination with the many Quranic references he constantly cited, made his argument seem bulletproof from my vantage point. Additionally, the guy seemed to have the contacts to make this trip happen. For him it was not even a question of pondering whether to go or not, it was a foregone conclusion that he would as soon as his time behind the walls came to an end. Me, I started to slowly but steadily move in that same direction. What else was I supposed to do upon release in a few months? Go back to my old neighbourhood and hope to find a minimum wage job? If those were even available right then for someone fresh out of prison. Or should I go back to selling enough amounts of drugs to be able to contribute to my household? That wasn't even a distant option since I had come to realize how morally reprehensible that was since it went against my religion. I couldn't even put that type of money on my mother's kitchen table after my transformation. Speaking of my mother, one of my most, if not the most embarrassing and shameful moments in my life happened at this time.

My correspondence with my family had been very sporadic during my prison stint. In the beginning I used to call mom a couple of times a week and at the same time talk to my sister if she was at home. As the weeks went by I called less frequently, there just wasn't that much to talk about to be honest. My mother was doing the same old thing, working hard and keeping her head above water, my sister was doing her own thing but was always very cautious of telling me details about her personal life (understandable teen behaviour). As for me, there wasn't really much for me to say. It's not like prison life was exciting and they didn't need to know that they had added raisins to the oatmeal one week or that I had picked up a job scrubbing the floor on our tier in order to have a little more money for commissary. It was mostly painful to talk after a while, I could hear it in my mother's voice. So it was natural to minimize the time we spent talking over the phone and it got reduced to calling every now and then, saying I miss you and I love you out of courtesy. My contact with my brother had not been much better, it consisted of letters that would be exchanged every three weeks or so. For a long time those letters didn't really contain any interesting information. Just the regular banter that the two of us were used to. How is it going? What are you doing? Any news? We were just keeping in touch. We were pretty close as brothers, but when you are both locked up there just isn't that much to say as both are aware that the other is going through the same shit as yourself. Then the crazy thing happened, I received a letter in which my brother was saying that he had become religious. He had started praying and learning new things about our faith. They had a Muslim study circle at his prison every week which he attended together with a group of other Muslim prisoners. They also had the privilege of having a Muslim chaplain that worked there and helped them out during these study sessions. That letter reached me during my last few weeks with Musa. I was thrilled to hear that from my brother and shared my joy with Musa who I could tell was genuinely happy for both me and my brother. We had both found our way back to Islam after being lost and divorced from it throughout our entire youths. I replied to that letter after a few days, expressing my happiness at the good news. I also told him that I, too, had started getting serious with Islam and that I had a good brother as my cellmate that was teaching me all these things. The next letter from him didn't reach me until I had Taymour as my new cellmate and Taymour's slick propaganda had already started taking root in my mind. My next response to my brother was not as warm as my previous one, it was lukewarm at best, and it would get worse from there, but back to my mother first.

At first I was obviously excited to tell my mother about my newfound connection to our faith. Ever since I was little I could remember it being a very important thing for her, in her own way many times, important on a personal level. Its import then seemed to increase with the things that our family had to put up with and I'm sure that it had even more meaning for her at the time my father got sick and perhaps even more so when he finally passed away. It started out with me telling her one day in one of our few and far between phone conversations that I had started praying and that I even tried fasting. I could sense the joy in her when she heard this news coming from my mouth. She had never really seen me pray, or for that matter even show low levels of interest in our faith. So to hear that I had started praying regularly must have been a form of confirmation that her own prayers had been answered, since I'm convinced that me becoming a better Muslim had been a constant theme in her invocations to Allah. Like I mentioned earlier, we didn't talk often over the phone and the next time we did I don't think I mentioned anything that had anything to do with Islam or my adherence to it. The time after that I had already started becoming swept into Taymour's twisted version of Islam and I felt uneasy about how I should interact and relate to other Muslims. His whole worldview was based on us being morally superior to everyone else, including of course all other Muslims who didn't accept his version of Islam, since they were (as was made clear to a sickening degree) our worst enemies. Mind you, at this time I did not see it as Taymour's worldview, rather it was the Quranic worldview, i.e. how God wanted things to be. When you are convinced that you have God on your side you don't care who you go up against or who you are insulting or attacking (which obviously makes religions, not just Islam, a dangerous weapon when it ends up in the wrong hands). That was the reason I wasn't ashamed when I one day, as my religious insanity was still peaking, I scolded my mother over the phone for not being a proper Muslim. I know, it sounds sick… and it truly was. If Musa was the person that opened up the gates to my religious awakening, then Taymour was the one that pulled me into my religious psychosis. I was praying, reading the Quran, and I had developed plans to one day join these warriors of God and fight our enemies in Syria and Iraq. I was, in my own mind, one of the very best Muslims walking on earth, and Taymour reassured me of this. Never mind that I was looking down on others, thinking that I was better than the next man, had hate in my heart, was sitting in jail, had sinned more than most people walking this earth. These things I was either oblivious to or I just thought that they were things in my past that had no importance any longer. I was too arrogant to see the many faults that had crept into my soul by adopting this Taymourian ideology and too confident that my past mistakes were totally forgiven due to this new path I was on. I was blinded by my extremism to the point that I thought I had the right to talk to my mother in the despicable way that I did.

I remember that I started out by pointing out that her prayers were not accepted if she didn't fulfill certain other obligations. One of them being leaving America and relocating to the Muslim lands (which in our mind was constricted to parts of Syria and Iraq where this pseudo-caliphate had been established). The migration to this caliphate and pledging allegiance to it was what the entire project was all about. I came to realize it even more after I came over here. They make it sound like the pledge is more important than the obligation to pray and do pilgrimage. So there I was, lecturing my own mother about migration to the true Muslim land. I'm telling this to a woman who was born in a Muslim majority country and fled to America. I could tell that she was put off by this talk about migration, she basically brushed it off, probably thinking that I was tripping or that something sudden had come into me that would vanish as fast as it had made its appearance. She reiterated how happy she was that I had begun praying and that I still held on to that practice. She also reminded me that Ramadan would be coming up and she told me what she had planned with her friends. She and her group of Muslim lady friends would always do it big every year during Ramadan. They would alternate each evening, having each other as guests at their houses and it would be a proper feast each day at sundown. When it was held at our house there were always leftovers that we could live on for a few days. I remember her saying back then, half jokingly/half seriously, that the food was only for those that actually fasted. A slight jab at us youngsters who never were strong enough in our faith to fulfill that religious duty. It was a subtle motivational tactic that never worked. Instead the food would end up being our lunch the next day. When she mentioned it over the phone that time I could hear on her intonation that she was hopeful that I would actually fast for the first time. Rudely, I brushed the conversation aside, returning to the topic of helping our Muslim brothers and sisters in need in Iraq and Syria. She was patient with me but I could tell that I didn't get through to her. Instead I asked about my sister and told mom to be harder on her when it came to wearing the hijab, the veil, and that she shouldn't let her daughter walk around out there in those streets uncovered. The question of the veil was always highly personal to my mother and I could tell that she wanted no part of a conversation where her son was lecturing her about something that was very special to her and had been one of her great struggles in life. We ended that phone conversation on a bad note. To me that was just a result of her not understanding where I was coming from. She could not perceive my perspective and it frustrated me. This new insight I had received should be understood by every single Muslim if they wanted to be saved from damnation and gain God's highest reward. How could she not see this? I didn't want her to be like most of the common Muslims in our country. Work, pray, fast and think that they are on the right path just because they are fulfilling a few obligations while living a rather calm life. I felt like, even though the conversation had ended on a bitter note, that I had carried out my obligation by at least informing her of this important thing that she was not apparently at all aware of. It is lately, within the last couple of months that I have realized what a tremendous sin I committed by talking to my mother in that way. My shame can't be described in words and this might be the only apology I can convey to you if it in some miraculous way reaches you mom. I'm sorry, I was wrong and write this with tears in my eyes. Please forgive your son who at that time didn't know better.

I would have let the tears flow if it wasn't for the two other people present in this room right now. They would probably look at me, thinking: what's wrong with this guy? Then most likely assume I was scared of the impending doom we are facing, and it wouldn't be out of the realm of possibility that they would take a coward like that out of his misery.

Then it was my brother. Like I mentioned, we found our faith that had been lost or perhaps dormant for so many years, at pretty much the same time. He started communicating a little more than usual after that by writing a few more letters. We never talked on the phone by the way. I obviously couldn't call him collect since we both made our outgoing calls from payphones. The other option was to use the cell phones that people smuggled in. Musa used to tell me about the cell phones the uncles used and how they could be had for the right price. Taymour also had some phone that he used that wasn't the payphone. The types of calls that guy was making couldn't be made over payphones because of the paranoia of them being tapped. Taymour had it somewhere else though, or with someone else and not in our cell. When it came to my brother it didn't matter much. Letters were fine. Sometimes, when you really miss someone it is easier to just write and not hear the voice, at least for me it's like that. It also has the advantage of being permanent in the sense that you can read the words over and over again as long as the letter is in your possession, as opposed to conversations that evaporate instantly and you can only think back on them while not being able to recall them verbatim. I felt the same about my mother but with her it was different since I sensed that she needed to hear my voice. Written correspondence worked well for both my brother and I, though instead of the former bland standard exchanges, the content started being more religious with each letter. My responses also started to become more religious in their content, yet I didn't know quite how to relate to him since he might be of the "others" that Taymour, me and the neo-caliphate could not be associated with. In one letter he gave a bunch of book recommendations that he said I should look for in the library and tell the staff to try to order them if they were not already in the collection. It was a rather long list of books and I can't recall them all. I do remember that there was a book on there by Al-Ghazali, another one by Ibn Ata Allah, there was also some poetry and some other stuff. I ran the list by Taymour who scorned the list, saying that these persons were nothing but deluded and misguided Sufis. In his words, some of the worst heretics in the history of Islam. If you want to be misguided, these are the very best people to read and listen to since they will take you far left of the straight path. Taymour described the Sufis as a cancer within the international body of Muslims, whose only treatment was extermination, they could not be reasoned with. I could tell that Taymour had real hate for them. The only other time that I had heard him express those types of harsh and ruthless words about other Muslims was when he was talking about the Shia. The Shia were enemies like no others. He had more severity in voice when talking about the Shia Muslims than he did when talking about the non-believers. It made me think that the Sufis had to be almost on par with the Shia as far as our enemies went. This in turn made me write a few letters to my brother that I am also extremely ashamed of and if you read this my brother, please forgive me. You were on a straight path, if you are still on it, be steadfast. If you happened to slip, find your way back to that path, since I'm certain it will take you to the destination that you were hoping for. Unlike the one I took which took me nowhere but to the pits of perdition.

He replied to my first rebuke. I'm assuming that he must have been taken aback by my cruel tone when I denounced the Sufi authors that he was reading and my condemnation of the heresies that people like that were spewing. He came across as defensive in his tone in the letter where he replied to my objections. He was trying his best to tell me about the merits of these scholars and how their teachings had impacted thousands, if not millions of Muslims to be better believers and better people in general. They had a group of likeminded inmates at his prison that were all followers of this cult that had hijacked the pure religion of Islam. In my second reply I was even more aggressive in my censure of his thinking. Out of all the different strands of our religion, he seemed to have fallen into the trap of one of the most wicked. I had talked more to Taymour about that brand of Islam that my brother was professing and had gathered up new amunition that I could throw my brother's way in order to refute him and hopefully make him reconsider his stance. I didn't tell him much about my own views about Islam. Taymour had warned me to stay low key when it came to the rhetoric concerning the caliphate, Syria and Iraq. He was constantly worried that we were being monitored and that there was a possibility that our outgoing and incoming mail was being read by the authorities. So while my second reply was more severe, it still didn't reveal my own stance, it just made it clear that I was in direct opposition to my brother's. His second reply to my rebuking was much more laid back in tone and not even defensive. To his credit, he was mellow in his response to my second attack. In hindsight I would not have blamed him if he had returned my fire with that of his own. Instead he tried to downplay the gap between our ways of looking at the religion we had in common. He was trying to explain that there was room for a lot of difference of opinion in many areas of religious thought and practice, and the same held true for the political sphere according to him. This was all foreign to me as Taymour's entire discourse was based on following only the Quran and the sunnah, as well as establishing and expanding the caliphate. There was no negotiation that could take place when it came to these principles of Islam. These things were clear as could be according to Taymour and by extension, myself. This talk about diverse opinions, especially when it seemed to be coming from so-called scholars that had been misleading Muslims for centuries, sounded like a bunch of nonsense to me. He wrote that he wished the best for me and concluded with some lines that were prayers for both of us, our mother and sister, as well as the Muslim community at large. Even though I appreciated reading his words which undoubtedly came from a good place, I couldn't stop myself from thinking that there was no way that Allah would accept a prayer from someone that has taken a heretical path within Islam, or according to Taymour, a path outside the fold of Islam.

In my next letter, after thanking him for his prayers, I attacked him even more vehemently. Again, not a proud moment. The more I talked to Taymour and heard about, not only his ideas but also his future plans, the more convinced I was that it would be the path for me. Simultaneously I became more hateful of anything that stood in opposition to our group's thinking. My attack on this occasion was very personal. I beg your forgiveness if you read this, my brother, from the bottom of my heart. You were right in what you were telling me. Unfortunately I realized it when it was too late. He never replied to that letter and I don't blame him. People that are as snowed in as I was at that time don't listen to arguments. I think that for people in that mindstate it is largely emotionally driven and not necessarily rational. Therefore rational arguments, no matter how powerful, usually don't have any positive effect. On the contrary, it might (especially if the person feels threatened by the intellectual attack) drive the person even deeper into his extremism in order to create more distance to his opponent. I was already in the process of a deep dive and my brother not responding was probably for the better. He was probably aware of the saying: if you are arguing with a fool, he is probably doing the same.

At the time, I was arrogant enough to believe that it was a sign of resignation on his behalf. I had at that time stopped playing chess in the prison's general area (mostly because I had gotten tired of getting beat up all the time) and took the correspondence and the way that it ended as my first chess victory by way of resignation by my opponent. Now I realise that he was just taking the high road, a concept that I was not able to grasp at that point. The tragedy in all of it was that that was our very last form of communication with each other, we never talked again. I talked to my mother a few more times after that on the phone but it was fruitless and laborious. I wanted to talk more to her about my new ideas but I already knew by the way she replied to me in prior conversations that there was no point in bringing it up. She would think that it was only a delusion that had fallen upon her son in prison (and she would not have been wrong) and do her best to either argue against it or just dismiss it as crazy talk. Instead we fell into formal talk about weather and such, things that people talk about when there is nothing else worth discussing and no common ground. It was sad. I know that she was just waiting for me to be released so that she could see me eye to eye again after me being away for a very long time. I'm sure that she didn't think much about the ideology that I had momentarily professed over the phone. She probably thought that those political ideas would vanish from my mind as soon as I came home, just as fast as they had appeared while I was locked up. She never saw me again. There wouldn't be a coming-home party for me, though I'm sure that she had one planned. It was not her fault, rather I had my mind set on other things (bigger and better I thought) and never even made a pit stop at home before heading over to the warzone that was supposed to double as the promised land. I was determined beyond any doubt in my mind, no one would stop me.

Abu Salih - disgraced son and brother

October 23rd

Young body
with old mind

Dignity
I sold mine

My spirit
no sun shine

Many trials
I load nine

Bad hustle
a slow grind

You think you got
goldmine

Witness killings
blown mind

Get used to it
go blind

Condolences
be fine

When it's my time
no shrine

That is the first time I ever tried to write anything that resembles poetry. I wrote it down on a piece of cardboard this morning, watching the sun go up through the blinders of what I assume was a living room window not long ago. It was spontaneous, I just wrote it in the moment. I started getting interested in poetry in the book club. At first I just looked at it as snobb literature. The poets seemed to all be riding high horses, too prestigious to write in a language that was easily discernible by laymen. Poets seemed distant and often too abstract for me. I felt like they complicated things unnecessarily. There is a simple way to write and to express ideas which is also easily accessible to prospective readers, the poet forgoes this intentionally to confuse us and at the same time place themselves on a pedestal, far above commoners. That is what I used to think. I no longer subscribe to that thought.

Over the last few months, as I have been thinking over the situation that I find myself in and the choices and circumstances that led me here. I have come to realize that there are many realities that can not be expressed in straightforward, concrete language. I realized that the language the poets use has the power to express the sublime and mysterious. The things that we can understand in our core, yet not express intelligibly with everyday speech, those are the things that poetry can express. If the reader has the right perceptions, he will understand the insight that the author is trying to offer. If he is on a lower level of understanding he will see the poet's words as rambling that could be expressed in a more efficient way, missing out on the deeper meanings of a world that he is not yet able to discern. I had to give it a try, not in order to express some wonders from the depth of my perception, rather in order to try to experiment with the word structure. I never truly realized how incredibly difficult it can be to write when a structure in the form of a meter is imposed on you.

Perhaps I'm boring you with this type of talk. I need to get back to my story if I'm hoping to even have a chance to finish it before they finish us. Our partner went out to get food again. He didn't argue when me and the other guy here suggested that it was just better that he went again since he went the first time. No need for one of us to shave his beard just to head out on this mission. He seemed to be resigned to the fact that this was his lot. Hopefully he will be coming back soon. He left not long ago, but it seems like there is a small town much closer to us than we had anticipated. It shouldn't end up being the long suspenseful mission that it was last time he headed out. This time around it should be fairly quick, unless he gets caught. We should know momentarily.

Inside prison, I went from worse to worse. At the time though, I thought it was from good to better. I was accelerating in my downwards spiral. Interestingly enough, the speed broke the sound barrier in a time when you as a Muslim are supposed to slow down and reflect. The month of Ramadan. Fasting had been an enormous boost for my faith when I tried it out with brother Musa. It had elevated my perception of things to a whole new level and it had brought me an inner peace that was not known to me prior. What I noticed the first time I fasted was that when I was fasting, I was naturally motivated to do more good deeds. It was as if I could channel my energy to the right places, to the worship of God and seeking knowledge. All other things seemed to be insignificant in comparison. Keep in mind that the first time I fasted it was just a regular day. When Ramadan came upon us, an entire new type of energy seemed to flood my veins. It was more intense than the first time and it felt like it was not only inside of me but also outside, as if the energy was hanging in the air everywhere that I went. I wanted to do more and more as far as my Islamic practice was concerned. More prayer, more reading. Taymour had other plans. We obviously prayed our daily prayers and read our daily portion of the Quran, but outside of that there was not really any extra studies or discussions about philosophical intricacies like there had been with Musa. Instead, the only topic worth discussing was the caliphate and how we should make our way there. Nothing else mattered. All we really did was to pray together and talk about the project. There were some other Muslims in our cell block that were also fasting but we did not socialize with them. That would be against the rules. In retrospect it would have been so nice to hang out with those guys and share experiences with each other. The only memories I have of truly happy times during Ramadan was when I was young and there were things we tried to do with the family. But since I did not fast myself back then I didn't really fully partake. It's pretty sad (not in the sense that I'm feeling sorry for myself, but still) that someone that fell in love with fasting the first time he tried it, never got to experience a proper Ramadan of Muslim brotherhood. My first full month of fasting was with Taymour in prison while we were making plans to conquer the world by defeating the kuffar, one battle at a time. The second and last one was not that many months ago. That was after I had just realized that the people I had joined and had made into a de facto family were a bunch of savages with no hearts. I never got to reap the fruits of fasting for the entirety of the blessed month in good company and emerging as a better person on Eid-ul-Fitr. Instead I surfaced as a monster, not the finished product that I would become a few months later, but well on my way. I was still getting what I thought was the same spiritual high that I experienced with Musa but it was of a different kind. It took me a long time and a lot of reflection before I could differentiate. What I experienced the first time was light, it brought me higher and I started feeling a closeness to God that I had not felt before that. While fasting with Taymour it was a darker feeling, yet at least as intense in its strength. Instead of the gravitational pull having its epicenter in the knowledge of God and the acquisition of new knowledge, the pull was towards the scheme of the caliphate and its grandiose plans and the push was coming from Taymour, constantly navigating me in that direction.

After we had finished fasting the entire month I only had about roughly a month left before my release. Those last weeks were spent in preparation, both mental in order to get me in the right mindstate and also in logistical planning so that I would be able to join as soon as I was a free man. I didn't talk to my brother at all at this point. Though he did send me letters with greetings for Ramadan, including prayers for me and our family. In my pettiness I didn't respond. It was my payback for him not replying to the last letter I sent. Instead I just went on with my plotting. Taymour claimed that he had all the connections set up on the outside. He had given me an address, all I had to do was show up and present myself. The rest would be taken care of. Travel documents, tickets, contacts in other countries, details of the travel plans. Everything was supposedly taken care of. All I had to do was show up, then apply for a new passport and hang out with the group that I was destined to travel together with and then take off on the determined date when everybody in the group would have all their business in order. Seemed simple enough and almost too good and easy to be true. Taymour was plugged in and had been making moves the whole time. From the moment he had been arrested he had kept working on this project, or rather, *for* this project.

The last couple of weeks in prison was unbearable and agonizing for me. I was so hyped to go after this build up that had taken place over the last few months, culminating in Ramadan. Taymour's constant coaching and his intense pep talks put me in a frame of mind that gave me a severe case of tunnel vision. I had a goal, to reach the caliphate and then serve. That was the only thing on my mind. Fear was not a factor. I had never been in a warzone before and most normal people should feel some form of apprehension before diving in head first into a civil war in a remote part of the world that they know absolutely nothing about except for hearsay. The responsibility of fulfilling the duty suppressed any such fear and hesitation. What if it didn't work out and I would happen to be killed right away or apprehended? The promise of the rewards for the martyrs was enough to ward off any such fright. It was a non-losing proposition. If you dedicated yourself to this cause you could only win. Everyone on our side would medal, no matter his individual outcome. It was a great free agent pitch that they made and Taymour played the role of a savvy manager that took advantage of naive rookies.

Before I was released from the pen I said my goodbyes to

the people that I had known for the majority of my stay. They weren't exactly warm farewells that I gave and the responses were just as tepid. They had noticed that I had changed. During the last few months of my stay my interaction with anyone other than Taymour was at a minimal level. Only if absolutely necessary would I have anything to do with outsiders. There was just no point in having any contact with them unless it was out of necessity. There was still a level of human respect that I felt that I had to uphold to not seem like a total weirdo and loser, so I said bye to guys like Denard and the guys that were still there from the old book club. I had a long talk with Taymour the evening before my release. We went over the plans in detail. It was straightforward and simple. Just get to a specific apartment, whose address I was given by Taymour of course, and present yourself and the codeword that only I, Taymour and the individuals in that apartment were privy to. That was it. From that point on everything would be simple, he said. He told me that he would catch up with me within the confines of the caliphate as soon as his time was over in prison, which would be soon. I never saw him again.

There was one rule that could not be broken upon release from prison: don't visit your family, under any circumstances. That would be the perfect opportunity for the devil to derail the plans. The family could make you weak and they would without a doubt try to talk you out of it if they found out about the plan. That was the *best* case scenario. The worst was that they would go to the authorities and report you and possibly bring down the entire operation and everyone that was involved in it. There was no risk involved with me whatsoever. I had no intention or desire to visit my folks. My mind was already set on my goal. My mother knew I would be released sometime around the time that I actually was, but she didn't know the exact date. I feared that I would get weak in the knees if I saw her crying for some reason and that it could lead to me breaking. Breaking was not an option since I believed that the duty to join and fight for the caliphate was above all other duties, those towards one's family included.

So I did what I was told as soon as I got out, went to the address and gave the passwords… and I was officially in. It was a modest apartment in the city. It wasn't the slums but it was also far from nice. One could easily tell that there were all types of shady activities going on in that apartment building, which none of us was against since it made us blend in without any problems. There were three guys in the apartment when I got there. Two of them were my age and the third a little older, I never asked his age but would guess that he was in his early thirties. He was clearly the leader of the band and was the one with all the contacts. He was working his phone constantly, apparently on some type of chat that was encrypted beyond imagination, the most expensive and secure that there was on the black market. We didn't ask much about each other, as I'm sure everyone had been instructed by whoever it was that sent them to that place. Age was not important, where you were from was not important, where you came from was not important. Everyone had adopted a nom de guerre and government names were to be avoided at all costs. Essentially, everything connected to one's past was ancient history that would have no importance in the future. The only thing that mattered was the trip to the caliphate that laid ahead. Me and this other guy had to get our passports in order. That was one of the things that we were waiting for, the other was another couple of guys who were supposed to join us. Once that was in place we would proceed with the journey as soon as possible since by that time our leader, Abu Mujahid, should have everything set up, down to the smallest detail.

The days were rather repetitive, good thing for me that I was used to it at that point. We would mostly just hang out in the apartment. We would pray together when the time for that came and we would sit and listen to short sermons delivered by Abu Mujahid. He also had this thing on the computer, it was basically like YouTube but some bootleg version that you could upload things to that wouldn't pass the screening at YouTube headquarters. If you did somehow manage to upload to YouTube, it wasn't worth the risk of having the video traced back to you and have the authorities come looking for you. So this was some dark web type stuff he had access to and we were watching all these lectures and sermons that were delivered by scholars (I really should use quotation marks when writing scholars since I have realized that those preachers were nothing but the worst charlatans) directly from within the confines of the caliphate. They went on and on about the duty to join and to their credit, made great sales pitches. They painted the picture with the most beautiful of brushes. We were made to believe that we would step into Eden as soon we touched down. A place with no trials like the ones we were constantly facing in the West. No islamophobia, no oppression, no injustice. Everything operating under the rules of Islam. Wives were longing for our arrival, especially the arrival of those that would show prowess on the battlefield. Money was coming into the state at a fast and steady pace. New oil fields had been conquered during the last few months and had made the economy rise from very good to excellent. This understanding that we started developing was based on three or four preachers and "eyewitnesses" that had been brought forth to testify from the civilian population. They too were gushing about the amazing conditions in the society ever since the caliphate took over. Little did I know at the time that these civilians were threatened with corporeal punishment if they didn't provide positive testimony for the administration that they could then broadcast. It might sound strange to you, but the tactics worked. We were all getting stronger convictions each day. Not only because of these types of propaganda videos but also by being around other like-minded guys who had the same aspirations as oneself. We started to develop a "us against the world" mentality in that apartment that resembled a war bunker more and more each day.

After a couple of weeks or so the two final members of this emigration squadron arrived and so did the passports which we had been waiting for with great anticipation. We were now six prospective soldiers in total with strong determination and the means required to make the trip. I still hadn't talked to my mother and sister, for all they knew I was still locked up and not in the mood to make a collect call. We didn't pack much at all. Everyone basically just had a backpack filled with necessities, enough cash to make it to our meet-up point if we were to get derailed. Most importantly we all had a determination that was stronger than steel, as well as a conviction that we were fulfilling the destiny that God wanted for the world.

Groups composed of members with that type of mindset are usually hard to stop.

We took off from JFK and landed at Heathrow. That's London, England, for those of you in America that happen to read this and haven't crossed the Atlantic. We had a very short layover at Heathrow (nice airport by the way, good job guys) and then we boarded a flight to Sofia, Bulgaria. That might seem kind if random to you and you might suspect that we stopped by a gymnastics competition on our way to the caliphate. That was not the case. The idea behind flying to Bulgaria was that Abu Mujahid (and whoever it was above him that was calling the shots for our jihadi armada) had a lot of contacts in Turkey. Turkey borders Syria and Bulgaria borders Turkey. The land route was the most secure, according to our intel. To fly directly to one of the bigger airports in Turkey would be a bad move. Their intelligence agency was looking hard for prospective adherers to the caliphate. Around this time there was a significant influx of foreigners to the caliphate from many different European countries, less from North America, but not negligible (I'm assuming that the influx has slowed down considerably lately due to the large amount of losses that the caliphate has been accruing). The largest torrent was from the surrounding Arab countries, the difference with the recruits from those countries was that they seldom used the Turkey route. Many European countries were working together with the Turkish authorities. Who of course had their own interest in the escalating conflict, in order to try to stop citizens from France, Belgium, the UK, etcetera to join up with the caliphate. This meant it was a bad idea to show up at Istanbul's airport, six deep with backpacks on, basically having a note on the forehead that said: I have never been here before. It would be the equivalent of trying to smuggle drugs across the Mexico-California border in a stolen Camry with N.W.A booming from the speakers and everyone dressed in gang attire.

Considering the risk, I have to say that our trip went smooth. On the planes we sat far away from each other. Deliberately booking tickets on seats that were not adjacent to each other. At the airports we never moved in a group, only as individual tourists. All communications were handled over an encrypted app that everyone had on their respective phones. We sat in two separate cars as we crossed the border and entered Turkey. The checkpoint was not an issue. We had contacts. If we went at the right time and used the correct lane we were guaranteed to make it through. We did stop for a second in Istanbul in order to rest and resume the journey the next day. Beautiful city I must say. I could write about that city for a few pages but I will spare you since I have more important matters to write about. Just take my word, or look for a YouTube video or something if you want to get a feel for what I saw in my short stay there. We switched to a new set of cars and also new drivers as we took off in a south eastern direction. The plan was to do the same when we reached Ankara. Obviously we didn't all fit in one car, though we could have used a minibus of some sorts but the idea was that if one vehicle got busted, the other one could continue. Not all eggs in one basket type of thinking. The long drive was rather boring to be honest. We had a driver who doubled as a preacher and was trying to boost our morale as we moved along the Turkish countryside. There was no doubt who was providing him with his paycheck. We would stop to pray and use the restroom. Other than that we just sat patiently in the car and waited. It was almost torture the way we were anticipating the entry into the caliphate. We had been visualizing this moment for so many months. It was a vision of a glorious future that we had replayed in our minds' eyes as we had built up the determination to join the project. Sitting in that car, looking out the window at the barren Turkish land, was a surreal feeling. We could feel the closeness of the caliphate. We almost reverted to small children asking the driver: are we there yet?

As evening was approaching we arrived in one of the border towns. The two carloads met up and the cell was reunited. The two drivers bid farewell, but not before putting us in contact with the driver that would take us across the border in a minibus. The danger of being busted was no longer existent. In my mind the border crossing would be much more spectacular and exciting. I had imagined some sort of tunnel that had been dug that ran right beneath the Turkish-Syrian border, that we would have to crawl through like some navy seals. Apparently the driver was going to take us over the border on one of the side roads. Even though we were in Turkish territory at the moment, it was in actuality controlled by the caliphate. We were going to wait until it got dark and then the coast would be clear. This is where I understood for the first time that politics were involved in this ordeal. From a practical standpoint, we could have just crossed the border in broad daylight and joined our faction on the other side. There was nothing that could or would stop us, but apparently people had to save face. And by people I mean politicians on each side of the conflict. Turkish politicians, Syrians politicians, and of course politicians of the many allies that these countries had. If it would be shown in the media that recruits were just waltzing in unimpeded it would be a PR nightmare. You might think that it would be good promotion for the caliphate's cause but it would most likely have the opposite effect. It would bring more attention which would require the caliphate's opposition to throw in a bunch or resources in order to not look like they are being dominated and controlled in this area by a state that is not even recognized as a state. Once that would happen, things would get tougher for the caliphate. The thing was that those resources were better spent in other areas according to the politicians of the respective countries. Therefore it was more pragmatic to accept the situation and look the other way while doing a discreet handshake under the table. I know, it seems absurd. The political side of this whole situation would get even more absurd the more I found out about it, but I will get to that later if time permits.

We entered official caliphate territory sometime around midnight, I think. There was a group of guys in military apparel that welcomed us and placed us in a couple of jeeps that took off. We rode for a few hours in the middle of the night until we reached something that resembled a camp. It was lit up in the middle of the dark night and very quiet and resembled some sort of big compound consisting of many brick buildings. There were guards on the perimeter that controlled the surroundings. We were ushered in and made to sit in something resembling an office and this guy dressed as some sort of general walked in and welcomed us. We all had to line up and approach his desk one by one. He filled out a form for each one of us. We had to tell him our names and other relevant information, which was checked to see if it coincided with our passports. Abu Mujahid spoke up and gave him the name of someone that I had never heard before, who must have had some kind of high rank within the organization since the general seemed to relax a little as soon as he heard the man's name. They were extremely wary of infiltrators and when Abu Mujahid mentioned his contact's name it must have signaled to the general that we were nothing to worry about, we had arrived through a secure channel. When our information had been registered we were told to sit down. The general took all our passports and put them in a plastic bag which he placed in one of the drawers in his desk. It hit me at that moment that it was *for real* now. I had always been all-in since I made the decision to go, but when I saw him put away our American passports in that bag I realized that there was truly no turning back. We were given instructions about the rules at this training camp. The training would take at least a month before we would be dispatched to the capital of the caliphate and the administration there would decide exactly where our military efforts were most needed at the moment. The war was at that time fought on multiple fronts at the same time so there was no telling where one would be placed.

We were shown our rooms where we would sleep. It was very modest as we lay close to each other on mattresses on the floor. We had a few hours to rest before the dawn prayer so we all went to sleep as soon as we could since training would start after breakfast, which was served closely after the conclusion of the prayer. When the morning light hit the camp it dawned on me what type of place this was. This was a true military training ground. Everything inside the compound was set up for training. There were shooting ranges, different types of obstacle courses for physical training and an area for hand-to-hand combat. Explosives were used outside the compound, a few miles out in the desert. Explosions could be heard all throughout the day in irregular intervals. There was not a woman in sight at that camp. The idea of marrying a woman dedicated to the caliphate's cause or claiming a concubine taken as war booty (honestly, that was not meant to be a pun) would have to wait until we got settled down in one of the cities. The training program they had set up for us was vigorous and very structured. Every day had a schedule that had to be followed to the letter. Everything was centered around the prayer times, so the different sessions would be set up around the congregational prayers, all of which were obviously mandatory to attend. They took good care of us. We had really good food to eat for breakfast, lunch and dinner. We were given clothes to wear and accessories which would come in handy in the future. They knew that many of us had left our homes with nothing but what could fit in a small bag. We also received firearms as soon as we had passed that part of the training and could prove that we could handle handguns and automatic weapons. These arms would become more beloved than children to some of the guys. A personal gun or assault rifle could become really personal and an attachment would develop for some after having used the weapon for what was perceived to be a noble cause.

Classes were conducted regularly throughout the training camp. It was really just more indoctrination. The same types of lectures that each one of us had already heard in our respective homelands. This time around it was delivered by more authoritative figures as they presented us to teachers who were supposedly the most learned in the world. It was a lot of doctrine that was taught, what differentiates us from them was constantly emphasized. What made us different from the obvious unbelievers was clear and needed no repetition. Instead the emphasis was placed on what made us people of the truth and the other "Muslims" people of falsehood and hellfire. Additionally we were also constantly reminded of the importance of our pledge of allegiance and what it meant. It was a commitment for life that could not be broken. If it was, there was only one punishment that fit the crime which was execution for high treason. Anyone that betrayed the bond he had made with God through the vicegerent, the caliph, would have to be put to death without unnecessary delay. The point stuck with all of us. We were already convinced, but after the repetitive lesson our convictions reached new heights.

There was one thing early on that threw me off, that I did not expect at all. The second day of camp I saw a group of children. There might have been around fifteen of them and they were going through their own training sessions. It took some time until I finally understood what they were doing as they stood in a line and waited their turn to learn punches. Or so it seemed. On closer inspection I saw that they were practicing stabbing with knives and the object which I had at first assumed was some sort of punching bag turned out to be the propped-up torso of a corpse. I almost vomited in my mouth but managed to hold back the gag by looking in a different direction. I was not ready for something that graphic.

I asked one of my training buddies about it and he seemed to think that it was completely normal. If we are going to fight the unbelievers we must also train the next generation to do so. It was the natural evolution of warfare and the expansion of the caliphate. Some of the kids were children of soldiers in the caliphate that were going through their military training, others were orphan war captives that were to be indoctrinated to serve the caliphate in the future. In my estimation the kids ranged from nine to thirteen years old. The explanation made sense to my at the time distorted mind, but something in my soul tried to tell me how repulsive it truly was.

The comradery in the camp was awesome. The brothers really bonded with each other. The common cause that we had all come there to fulfill made our so-called brotherhood very strong. We had brothers from the U.K., U.S., Belgium, Holland, the Scandinavian countries, former Yugoslavia, Germany. It was a cocktail of nations from the Western hemisphere. Most of us spoke English with each other, unless it was a Frenchman speaking to a Frenchman of course. Not a lot of Arabic was spoken even though some of us tried to force ourselves to speak Arabic in order to learn it faster. Even the leaders in the camp spoke to us mostly in English in order to make sure that they were properly understood. All the Arabs that had joined the cause were at a separate camp in some other region of the caliphate. Most of the Arabs that had joined from the immediate surrounding areas already had extensive fighting expertise and were in no need of the type of training that we had to go through. I learned later that for many of them it was much more financially motivated than it was for us. For the people that had the same background as

I did, the motivation was to a very large extent based on the ideological conviction. For many of the local Arab recruits it was not much more than a paycheck. Many of them came from areas that had been wartorn for many years already and lived on the brink of starvation. Joining was a pragmatic decision based on survival and providing for one's family. It was another one of the many political aspects of the entire war that I had no understanding of at that point in time.

After the training was over we were divided up and sent to different regions. I had the luxury of going to the de facto capital of the caliphate, a fate that many wished for. I went there in a military truck together with a few other newly certified soldiers. I had the company of one of the other Americans that I came with, which felt like a comfort. A couple of East African guys were also in that truck, they were from the U.K. and spoke a brand of English that was hard to understand. When they started talking fast and using slang they could just as well have been speaking Japanese. There were also a few guys from either Sweden or Norway, I can't remember. A few of them looked like Arabs and one of them was the blondest guy I have ever seen, blue eyes and everything. That guy was *super* excited. We were all excited and the adrenalin was flowing like the Nile, but the blond couldn't hold back. He went on and on about how he was going to kill unbelievers and then seek out martyrdom. During the entire ride to the capital the guy was energized as if on MDMA.

We reached the capital together with a few other convoys coming in from different locations. We were taken to some form of administrative center where large parts of the leadership of the caliphate was located. Where the actual caliph to whom we had sworn allegiance was to be found was not known to us and would become lore amongst the soldiers. He was in our very city, walking the streets like a regular citizen. He was in the army and at the frontlines right now. He was out of the country for his own safety while plotting our next move. Rumors were overflowing and the truth might only have been known by God himself. I know that I never saw the caliph with my own eyes during my stay. At the administrative headquarters they gave us keys to apartments. We got to share apartments, unless you had a family of course, then you would get your own spot. I got to share it with this guy from the U.K. He was this Pakistani guy who also talked with an accent but not close to as strong and unintelligible as the British guys in the truck. The apartment was modest and had most things one could ask for. Electricity that worked (it did when we moved in at least) and cold and hot water. It was fairly clean and looked sanitary. To us two that were coming from the U.S and U.K. respectively it was definitely a downgrade in standard and it also didn't match the lofty picture they had painted of the luxury that awaited us. Having said that, it was not bad for two very young bachelors and definitely well above the average compared to how other people lived in Syria and the surrounding areas that had been wrecked by war during the last few years. The neighbourhood seemed quiet and calm. Outside of the occasional Kalashnikov going off in the street and the car horns that seemed to sound off so often that it made you think that people were communicating through them in morse code. People weren't really seen out in the streets unless they were moving around to take care of necessities. A lot of the businesses had been closed down it seemed like. There seemed to be constant reports about how good life was under the caliphate on the local tv channel. Even some foreign reporters were let into the capital to conduct interviews with the citizens to see how their experience was under this new regime. It was all smiles and glowing reviews that were shown on the tv sets and on YouTube clips. Little did I know at the time, that every single smile on the lips of the locals were induced by fear and threats of severe punishment. On the surface it looked great and quite harmonious, which is what we were made to believe before leaving our home countries. That picture was indeed strengthened when we first arrived and couldn't see the problems that existed in the depths, not seen in daylight.

There was not much time to relax. Pretty much as soon as we got there we had to head to the battlefield. It must have been on the second or third day already. We had arrived in a time of intense fighting that was taking place on many fronts at the same time. This was after things seemed to always break in the caliphate's favour. For a while there, almost every news report stated that another town had fallen to the new power of the region, the self-proclaimed caliphate. The wind was in the back of the novel pseudo-state and no one seemed to be able to halt their expansion and push back this military power that appeared to have come into existence almost overnight. The tide turned however, like it eventually always seems to do. Enemy forces started fighting back more fiercely, at times with new backing of foreign powers. The caliphate had soldiers with strong convictions on their side but many of the opponents had fighters with long experience in the battle field. It was also, of course, a battle of resources.

The team with the strongest financial backing won the majority of the battles, so it led to an ebb and flow. So the period in which I arrived was one in which victories no longer seemed guaranteed and each battle was up for grabs.

There is nothing that can prepare you for war. Movies, video games, training camps, pep talks. None of it comes even close to giving you a taste of what will happen when you for the very first time stand there. Nothing will test your belief in what you are doing and your resolution as much as bullets flying past your head and explosions going off in your vicinity that make your intestines quake and make your esophagus contract. That is the moment that you find out if you are built for that life or not. Some are, and they often go all in and it becomes a main part of the rest of their life. Some aren't, and they will either die early on in the process or retreat to wherever it was that they came from, far away from the terrors of the battlefield. If there is one thing that I would speak out against, if God somehow miraculously extends my life past this impossible predicament that we are in right now, it is the glorification of war in movies, video games and music. Most of us (boys and young men) fall for the bait and look at what is being promoted as heroic, glamorous, prestigious and praiseworthy. It gets ingrained in our minds and beings with the movies and video games from a very young age. Then it continues for many of us as we get into rap music and the bravado lifestyle that is sometimes attached to it.

After having witnessed the things I have witnessed over the last few months I feel sorry for every child out there in the world that is innocently looking at a TV screen where dramatized war is being shown or holding a controller in his hand, with which he can kill at will some soulless opponent that will get a new life as soon as this virtual one is terminated. Real life on the battlefield is far from the fanciful ones we saw growing up. There is… I was going to write pain but pain is not a sufficiently accurate word for what is felt when limbs get torn apart and internal organs shatter. The sound coming out of grown men's mouths while laying in agony on the ground can not be described. It makes the most horrific soundtrack from your favorite scary movie sound like a lullaby. I have seen a thirty year old man cry and scream for his momma as he lay on the ground looking down on what is left of his right leg after having stepped on a landmine, while bleeding to a helpless death. I have heard more than one person beg for a mercy shot to the head after receiving rounds from an automatic weapon in the stomach, scrambling the intestines so bad that instant death was the only thing they could think of begging for. I have seen bullets fly through skulls and leave the victim lifeless faster than you would think it was possible for a soul to leave a body. One second the guy is talking to you in the trench or yelling out instructions in the field. The next he is laying there lifeless as if there had never been a sign of life in that body. In war, things happen fast and there are no do overs, no extra lives, no reset button. When things happen they happen *fast* and when they don't, time can move at a snail's pace and everything slows down as if we were part of some instant replay in a NFL game. You can actually hear bullets. I'm not talking about the sound that is made when they are fired, rather the sound they make when they cut through the air, mere inches from your cranium.

You can't imagine the feeling of letting rounds fly from an

automatic weapon in the heat of battle. Your fingers squeezing and holding the trigger while wrath pours forth through an anonymous barrell, taking off in the direction of the despised enemy who could be dead already by the time you realize that you hit the target. You can't imagine. You don't feel macho, you don't feel like a hero or a legend in the making. Instead you start pondering your own existence like you never did before. Who am I to kill? To kill some faceless opponent just because he is being called an enemy by your commander. Who was the person that I just sent to the next life? Did he have a family? Did he have a wife that was longing for his return from this military expedition? Did he have children that were crying, waiting for dad to come home and when he didn't, had to be weighted down by those tears for the rest of their lives? These, and many other questions come to you simultaneously as you shoot to kill and you ponder your own existence as you are carrying out orders coming from above that have to be carried out unless the accusation of treason should be cast on you. The thought of war is not comparable to the realities of war. The intensity of what you will feel when seeing things no human should see can not be encompassed by thought before actually experiencing that reality. You will see limbs severed and limbs twisted in directions they should not be able to bend. You have no idea how you will react the first time you see a body without a head or a body that has its head in place but doesn't have anything left below the abdomen. Your eyes will send signals of repulsion to your brain when you see dead children and even dead babies. Those signals will be converted into convulsions and uncontrollable vomit when you realize that you and your army were the murderers. What was their crime? I never received an answer to that question. Partly because I was too scared to ask it and partly because there probably isn't one, at least not one that will make sense to a healthy mind. Consoling yourself that you were tricked into killing or in essence threatened since you yourself would die if you didn't kill, does nothing to alleviate the inescapable daydreams and unavoidable nightmares. You still did it, rationalization be damned. Ever since I killed the first time I have dreamt about it *every* single night that I have managed to fall asleep. It comes back to you in different forms, different permutations. The lives you have taken get projected in your dreams like perverse movies that you can't turn off, reminding you of your sins every single time you fall asleep. The dreams become distorted and grotesque, almost like fever dreams that leave you sweaty, confused and exhausted when you wake up from them. I could go on and on about my nightmares but this is not meant to be a dream diary, just know that I have seen things while awake as well as sleeping, that no horror movie director could ever think of.

I wasn't the only one that couldn't stomach the realities of war. Many of us acted like lions waiting to be let out of our cages while we were at the training camp. Once let out and seeing what this was all about, turned into kittens looking for mama cat and her comfort, but there was no mama. She was left behind in the land of the unbelievers, disregarded as a lost soul that could not see the truth of the project of the caliphate. I got the sense that many felt like me in that regard, though not many at all had the guts to mention it to anyone. There seemed to be soldiers in each platoon whose motto was: I want it so much that it hurts, but when I'm allowed I don't dare. So much bark, much less bite. Showing weakness was not an option since it would in the very best case lead to harsh discipline. Instead we were left to process the dissonance we started experiencing by our lonesome selves. We didn't have the tools to do this. There was no army psychologist or chaplain one could go to and open up to about one's fears, the things one had done and regretted, one's recurring nightmares. Instead it was internalized and never properly processed. I (and I imagine many others) was carrying around enormous amounts of guilt, angst, anger, uncertainty and shame, along with a host of other emotions and psychological states. Since there was no proper outlet for all these things that were affecting our souls, it manifested itself in even more psychopathic behaviour, leading to a very negative spiral. For others it came in the form of depression and for some it came as a night visitor that reminded them of their past and ongoing sins.

My Pakistani roommate died on the battlefield and in my arms. It was a night battle. We were exposed to an ambush by our enemy that night and many on our side fell. As we realized what was going on we tried to escape right away. Me and my roommate thought that we would make it, as we saw the building that we were running towards for shelter and where we hoped to be able to hold off the enemy long enough, until our reinforcements could join the encounter. As we approached the building I could feel him falling in my periphery. He was running on my right side, slightly behind me, in full stride. I heard the sound that someone typically makes when getting punched in the stomach really hard and becomes incapacitated. I turned around and saw him lying face down on the ground, still moving his limbs. The darkness worked as a cover and I took my chances to rescue him. In reality that is what a true soldier is supposed to do, not leave their own behind under any circumstances. It sounds great in theory, it just doesn't work like that all the time when enemy bullets are flying around your head, explosions are going off and you are millimeters away from shitting your own pants. All you can think about at that time is extending your life and taking another breath. I knew that the enemy was just trying to get lucky as they let their automatics smatter in the pitch black night and that the odds of getting hit were probably much lower than what my stomach was telling me. I got down and just started dragging the Paki brother. He was grunting something unintelligible as I kept pulling him towards the door of the building. Once there, a guy from our squadron arrived and helped me to carry him up a flight of stairs. I dragged my wounded roommate to a corner of the room and sat down and leaned against the wall for a few seconds. I had to recover for just a little bit from the adrenaline high and the exhaustion that resulted from transporting this guy who with equipment on easily weighed over two hundred pounds. He was taking short, intense breaths that sounded heavy. I asked him where he was hit. He started rambling, pronouncing words that I couldn't understand, though I was able to pick out "back". I pulled up his shirt and he started letting out screams. I looked for exit wounds on the front of his torso but saw none. That had to mean that the bullets had penetrated his back and moved around within his upper body, tearing apart any organs that came in their way. The way he was breathing made me think that he had to have a punctured lung. Anytime I tried to move him in any type of way he would let out loud screams that pierced my eardrums. I assumed that he must have major damage to his internal organs. Perhaps a lacerated spleen, or liver, or kidney, a ruptured intestine… or all of the above. More and more guys were gathering in the building and after a while it was safe to assume that all those who did not get mowed down in the desert night had made it to the relative safety of that temporary shelter. Our injured companion sounded like he was having a harder time breathing with each breath that passed. I changed his position by lifting his head unto my legs as I sat on the ground. I figured that elevating his head might give him more open pathways for oxygen intake. I had no idea what I was doing, I was just acting on pure instinct. One of our companions approached us as I sat on the concrete floor with his head in my lap, listening to nonsensical utterances coming out from his lips. The guy kneeled down and looked at me, then shifted his gaze to our wounded companion. His eyes then travelled to the floor and locked in on something. I too started looking at the spot where the soldier's eyes had fallen and saw a growing puddle of blood beneath my injured roommate. The soldier looked the wounded Pakistani in the eyes and then looked straight into mine and simply told me: "He's done." He walked away and joined the others in the room who were busy calling on back up and trying to figure out how to escape from this ambush.

I tried to talk to my roommate to keep him in the present somehow but he was not responding. He kept on mumbling non-stop in Urdu with occasional expressions in Arabic sprinkled in. I heard prayers being said and a bunch of other stuff that I had no clue what it was. I could feel my legs slowly getting soaked by the blood that was emanating from his upper body. He was staring straight forward towards the ceiling as he kept rambling in what was turning into a whisper. He saw something in front of him that I could not see. His eyes were locked on some object that I myself could not perceive. He would not look away, his eyeballs big like lightbulbs. His mumbling was becoming inaudible and was finally reduced to just the movement of his lips. Blood started trickling down his cheeks as it made its way out from his mouth. He stopped breathing with his mouth agape and eyes still wide as the horizon. I'll never forget those eyes and the look on his face when his soul had left his body. Even if I wanted to forget it would not be possible since I am reminded every time I sleep. Just like I have regular nightmares of killings, gore, victims and such, I also get the recurring image of him dying in my arms. It comes back in different alterations every single time I fall asleep and have a dream. It always comes at the very end, right before I wake up. It's the last thing I see in my dream and the first thing I see when I wake up. Sometimes while dreaming I am aware that it is a dream and I hope to get out of it but can't force myself to wake up. When I get to the part of his dying face being shown to me it is a paradoxical moment as it is relieving to know that the dream is about to be over even though it's the scariest part of the dream. Then I have to wake up and face reality and it makes me think which is worse; the world of horrible nightmares or the reality of hell on earth?

I have wondered a lot about how many others struggle with the same type of haunting nightmares and visions. I have heard both my companions that I'm with right now going through some form of torture in their sleep. I can tell by the

way they move around sometimes as I sit here and write while they are visiting the dreamworld, also by the things they
sometimes say in their sleep. Their movements while sleeping
must mean that they are having very interactive dreams. To
the outsider not knowing what we are going through it must
look like an epeleptic fit. We never talk about it. It is like the
unspoken secret here I think. Everyone (or close to it) are
going through extreme psychological states bordering insanity, PTSD, some even psychosis. It can not be mentioned
though. It is easier to neglect it and pretend it does not exist.
It is not only easier, it is probably necessary for the survival of
the group. Since we are representing "the truth" and fighting
for it in the name of God, how can such negativity result from
it? To admit that it exists would be sowing the seeds of doubt
in the ideology, and that can never happen if you are destined
to take over the world.

October 24th

We will eat food for a few more days, in sha Allah. Our friend
came back from his latest grocery run. The good news is that
we have food and water that is palatable. We have tap water at this place but it leads to… let me spare you disgusting
bathroom stories. He came back with a couple of bags and a
lot of stress and paranoia. He also came in here looking like
someone that had just smoked way too much the way he was
moving his head and arms while telling us that he was sure

that he had been spotted. He said that they made him out at the store. He could sense people talking behind his back, pointing at him, telling those that would listen that he was one of the enemies. He also told us that we are even closer to the nearby settlement than we originally had thought. The guy ran to each window and peeped out to see if anyone was standing outside, he mentioned how he was sure that they had trailed him to the house. Me and the other guy looked at each other, not sure what to think of this guy's claims. It is easy to become paranoid when your life's on the line and you have been running for weeks, constantly trying to avoid the enemy. Having to constantly look over your shoulder and sleep with one eye open will drive you crazy for real. It wouldn't be outrageous to dismiss his nervous breakdown as mere delusion. On the other hand, if we didn't take it seriously it could mean that our end is much closer than we had hoped. I didn't know what to think and I still don't. We all started cleaning our weapons and making sure that we sat at good spots if they were to storm us and a firefight would break out. Nothing happened the first hour, we just sat there patiently waiting for the door to get knocked down or blown up. We sat there muttering prayers until we realized that they were probably not out there. We checked the windows several times and couldn't see any movement outside. We all relaxed a little bit after that. The guy with the nervous breakdown was still going on about it, he was adamant that they had identified him. He soon realized though that even if that was the case, there wasn't a whole lot he could do about it. I just went back to my writing.

After several misfortunes on the battlefield, things went

from bad to worse. Back in the capital the standard that existed when I first got there was slowly deteriorating. They also started dropping bombs which unfortunately affected the civilian population greatly. Electricity went out, the sewage system collapsed. A major hospital, which was already overloaded with injured soldiers, got hit. The soldiers always got prioritized for treatment. The civilians that were collateral damage could wait. Nurses and doctors were forced to work around the clock, forget about compensation. The welfare system that the caliphate was so proudly using to attract adherents and create goodwill with the local population slowly started getting usurped by the people in power. The facade was falling down and exposing the inner workings of the administration.

Many things led to my disillusionment with the project of the caliphate, but none more than how the administration acted. I'm not saying that every single official was corrupt. I'm sure there were a few honest ones that were actually sincere in what they were trying to accomplish, though completely misguided in their outlook. I am also of the belief that the honest ones have tried to abandon ship and repent or that they will very soon. As for the rest, I believe they were in it for their own good and not some greater cause. The greater cause was only important as long as it benefitted themselves. When money was flowing it was easy to be generous. It is much easier to give when your own pockets are overflowing. A different story emerges when the money flow gets constricted and decisions have to be made. When that happened, the first ones to suffer were the civilians and after them the people on the ground like myself that were doing the heavy lifting. The ones in the best houses calling the shots were hit last by the disaster.

I feel the worst for the civilians, the original residents of the capital, before this pseudo-caliphate claimed it on the pretense of making it the center of justice in the world. The city had already been through hell before the latest invasion and siege. It had been in the crossfire of the civil war for a few years already. None of the occupants were good. If you asked them to pick I assume that they would compare it picking amongst deadly diseases. In the beginning I could not perceive their discontentment. There were plenty of smiles, especially from business owners. At the time I didn't know that these smiles were motivated by fear of the intruders. Me being one of them of course. We walked around there in our military clothing and rifles hanging over our shoulders, thinking that the smiles we received were out of gratitude for us liberating them from being under the control of the regime. I couldn't have been more out of tune with what they really thought of us. We walked around there in the city, policing the inhabitants, telling them what was right according to God and what was wrong. All the rules directly derived from the lessons we had at the training camp and which we kept on having in the city. It never struck me that families would take offense when outsiders came and told them how to practice and understand their religion, when these same families had been Muslims for many generations and some even had great scholars in their lineage.

I met a local guy who was my neighbour, he was the one who told me how we were perceived. This was not even that long ago and it was a short while after I had realized that I had fallen in their trap and made a pact with the devil himself. His name was Rashid, he was this scrawny youngster. He was a computer wizard apparently. He was one of the natives in this city and was part of an underground movement that had as its goal to expose the caliphate's inner workings to the outside world. Any videos and pictures that made their way out of the caliphate and were broadcasted around the world, were done so by the permission of the administration. It was all planned. When journalists were let in they were handpicked and what they were allowed to show and who they were allowed to interview was all carefully supervised. Rashid made it his goal to show a different side, the *real* side. He posted pictures and videos and wrote articles. He showed the devastation that the caliphate had caused, directly and indirectly. He interviewed people who for obvious reasons remained anonymous. He showed the direct consequences of the occupation on the economy. Families who were living a good life, running a family business before the occupation, were now forced to beg for food on the outskirts of the city while hiding from the morality police. He showed what life was like without electricity and clean water in the pipes. He showed the disgusting effect of a sewage system that had collapsed. He also pointed out the idiocy of recruiting a multitude of soldiers while neglecting people with expertise in plumbing, electricity, sanitation, and so forth. The caliphate's propaganda machine always tried to use bombings and such to their advantage by always blaming the regime and their allies. In other words they tried to spin it in a way that absolved them from blame for anything that happened and tried to instead use it as a recruiting tool. Rashid was there to provide the counter narrative. I respected this guy a lot the more I got to know him. He had the chance to flee from the oppressive rule of the caliphate but instead chose to stay and keep on fighting internally. He told me that not long ago his former roommate and a few others came up with a plan and managed to escape. They managed to slip out, thanks to good planning and some craftiness. Those days were over he said, those types of escapes were a thing of the past. A not very distant past at all, yet not plausible to revisit at this current time. One would think that as the caliphate was becoming weaker and weaker, that escaping would have become easier. On the contrary, they have become extra attentive when it comes to deserters. Or in their minds. traitors, betrayers and apostates. People leaving the cause was one of the biggest hits to the image of the caliphate. Not only did it show weakness, some of the people leaving had access to classified information that the administration definitely didn't want to leak out.

There was a wave of women that tried to flee, in many cases together with their children. Some of them had been widowed while in the early stages of pregnancy and birthed children within the confines of the caliphate. After becoming disillusioned themselves they realized that there were only two options. Stay and let their kid (or kids) be raised by the next jihadi in line to pick up an extra wife or escape and hope to make it out and get a new chance in life in some other country, perhaps even from the one that they fled from. The destiny of those caught while trying to run was not one filled with mercy. The men were imprisoned while waiting for a mock trial. Most of the time it seemed to lead to public executions. The women were often enslaved and treated like concubines. They were considered apostates through the act of trying to desert and then became de facto non-Muslim POWs that could be taken as slaves. In essence their lives would turn into the same as that of the many Yazidi girls that were captured and forced into servitude. The upper class in the caliphate acted with greed as they collected harems of maids that became their legal possession. I was approached about acquiring one, by way of purchase. My dreams of finding a wife in this place had crashed and burnt... and we all have our needs. I couldn't do it though. It was impossible for me. I was disgusted by the thought of being with a woman against her own will, no matter what concessions the reigning law offered us. I did think about "buying one" just to save her and her child too if she had one. Not even touch her, just let her stay in the apartment and protect her from being bought by someone else who would put her through hell. Things fell apart for myself though about the same time and I wouldn't even have the means to support her like I wanted too.

The war kept on raging and we went from one mission straight to the next. There were only very short intervals of time, a few days tops, when we could stay home and recover before heading out on the next mission. In those few days of "free time" I tried to hang out with Rashid without being seen, in order to expand my understanding of the lie that I had bought, ate and swallowed.

Our relationship developed after a very slow start. A slow start that was very understandable. He could see that I was a soldier and a foreigner and I could see that he was a regular civilian. I started out by just being cordial whenever we ran into each other in the stairways or right outside the apartment. I didn't want to scare him away. I knew that if I came on too aggressive he would probably suspect me of trying to fool him and eventually report him to the authorities. He had every right to suspicion, based on what he had seen the occupying force do to his hometown. He had also been in contact with people that had been a part of the caliphate, even some that had high positions in the administration, and helped them to get out of this phony state. This might sound cheesy, but I think he could see it in my eyes. They must have been the eyes of someone who was defeated. Tired of killing, tired of destruction, tired of suffering, tired of the lies. My face was probably a dead give away. I held up a mask around my colleagues and still do it to this very last moment, but when I'm by myself I remove all the makeup.

Rashid was brave. He took a chance on me. I could have been someone pretending and who later on would report him for his underground activities and online attacks against the state. He was a very determined person though. The capital was his hometown. He refused to flee. He could have been in a different part of Syria if he wanted to or perhaps even in some other country. Like neighbouring Turkey for example or even hit gold and reach the promised land of most refugees; Europe. He wasn't about to escape from his own hometown that helped raised him just because some cowboys in Muslim disguise had occupied it. He was going to fight his battle from the center of the city and either go down in flames with the town or be there as a proud survivor once the caliphate had run away and vanished.

I started visiting him in his modest apartment. He was living in it by himself for the moment after his last roommate had made a run for it and made it out alive. It wasn't the cleanest place but also not bad. I could tell that he had other things that preoccupied him and that apartment maintenance was not the top priority. It made sense since the apartment could get pulverized any minute if one of the many bombs found its way there. To be fair it looked better than any other bachelor's apartment I had visited in the capital. The ones that had the cleanest places were the ones that had "maids" living with them. Those apartments were spotless, but many of us did not indulge in that form of luxury. He had his laptop set up on the coffee table in the living room in front of an old beige sofa. I could tell that that was where he did his work and his damage. He was like a silent assassin with that machine in front of him. He gave the term keyboard warrior a real meaning. This guy was a youngster but started acting as my de facto shrink. He had heard enough crazy stories (and experienced many himself) to be able to actually give you some feedback when you talked, he didn't just sit there and look sad as tragedies were told to him. It took a little while until we got there though. The first times we sat together we didn't get too personal. We mostly made smalltalk. It wasn't the case that I was not ready to open up, it was just that I had *so much* moving around in my mind that I didn't know where to start. It was relaxing though to sit with someone that I knew was not a caliphate proponent and at the same time didn't fear me. It made even the otherwise meaningless chatter fill an important role, it became the first form of (much needed) therapy.

He started to tell his story from the beginning and I started feeling pity for the youth. I say youth, it wasn't like he was much younger than me. We never discussed age, for all I know he could even have been a couple of years older than me. He looked like a boy though in his simplicity and with his youthful face. Me on the other hand, I felt old. I had seen destruction and been the cause of it. I had done many wrongs already in a very short time in this land… I had killed. He was opening up about himself and also told me about the suffering that had been endured by the locals, and continued to be endured in the very moment that we were speaking (and most likely still while you are reading this). He gave me a lot of background info about the war and a short history lesson about the current conflict. That in itself was eye opening for me. The war and all the internal conflicts related to it were extremely complex. I had been told that, before coming over and during my stay, that it was the government that was oppressing the people and that Shia Muslims (even though people within the caliphate did not refer to them as such since they were excluded from the fold of Islam completely) were killing fellow Sunnis. It was a simplistic explanation that was reaffirmed in the beginning stages of fighting, if you were willing to limit your perception to the surface. That the current Syrian regime was the biggest crook in the conflict was agreed upon by all apparently, Rashid included. Outside of the regime there was a large collection of different groups who all were culpable and had a responsibility for the suffering of the civilians. Foregin actors as well; America, Russia, Turkey, Iran. Everyone seemed to have a vested interest in how the power structure in the region should be molded going forward and did what they could to promote their own priorities.

The caliphate was not the first group that claimed to be rescuers that would liberate the locals from the oppression of the current overlords. Everytime it seemed to be the same thing. The new conqueror is promising the removal of oppression and the establishment of just rule. Either they wither away before they can establish anything substantial or they turn out to be hypocrites or people deluded enough to believe that what they are imposing on the people can be called justice. It was the same thing over and over again, no matter what the group in question called themselves or what brand of justice they claimed to be representing. The thing about the caliphate that perhaps rubbed the civilians the wrong way more than anything else was their arrogance. They alleged that they stood for and spoke for some type of pristine form of Islam that had been absent from the world since the earliest days of the religious communty's existance. This in itself was not a noble claim, it echoed what most reformist groups say about themselves, even recognizable across religious boundaries as similar phenomena exist in Christianity and Judaism, etcetera. What made this new group, who simultaneously pretended to establish a state (the modern state being a very modern and secular concept mind you, the irony is not lost on me at this moment) was to enforce their version of Islam on the locals with severity. It is one thing to be argumentative and fierce in a debate about a religious topic. It is a different thing to threaten subjects with corporal punishments if they don't listen and obey. The thing that hurt the most for many Syrians like Rashid, was that they had themselves been the product of a long history of Islamic traditions that had scholarly roots. It's not like the caliphate was trying to convert people who had lived isolated in some remote area of earth who needed to be civilized and taught the proper creed in order to attain salvation. Rashid and the ones like him, men and women, knew their religion very well. Their societies were not perfect, far from, but exponentially better than the barbarism that was thrust upon them by these new intruders. Many of which had no idea at all about the history of Islam in Syria.

One day, after we had built up more trust for each other, he brought an acquaintance to his apartment when I was there. This was not long ago, only a few months. I would visit Rashid as often as I could during the times I was at home. Fighting was really intensifying so we would go from one battle to the next with only very short stops in the capital to regroup. It was fairly easy to visit Rashid since we were in the same building. Otherwise it would have been a mission to go to and from his place undetected. Caution was still important though since ears and eyes existed everywhere. This one day he brought this guy, also rather young looking, perhaps late twenties or very early thirties. He had red hair and a red beard that hadn't been trimmed in a long while. He had these greenish eyes, his appearance made him look as if he was from the British Isles. He was a scholar, apparently, who had been taught in one of the ancient universities in Damascus and then returned to his hometown. If I had seen the guy on the street I would never have thought about him being anyone of prominence. He shook my hand and looked me kindly in the eyes. I was wary due to my earlier experiences. When someone was called a scholar I became suspicious right away. The first "scholar" I trusted made me travel across the world to become a murderer and the ones I listened to after that guided me deeper into destruction. Now this guy, who didn't even look like a scholar. Or rather, not like I supposed that a scholar should look. Maybe that was the thing, I had been way too fixated on appearance. To be religious, you had to look the part. The complete opposite had been proven to me over the last few months while living with animals that claimed to be pious believers. So why not give this guy a chance?

He asked me about my background and I told him much of the same that I had told Rashid before, while adding new info about my journey to both of them. Ali, which was his name, could tell right away that I had been tricked. That I had close to no knowledge about the religion and had gone through trauma before my psychosis became apparent to him and he explained that it was a common denominator for many that had gone through the same transformation as I had. The guy seemed to be able to relate to what I was saying and listened attentively. I opened up quite a lot, I had to. There was so much sadness and frustration that had built up inside me that I was at the verge of exploding if I did not let it out. I was also continually going to war in the battle fields and each time it led to more trauma and more haunting nightmares. Ali and Rashid listened patiently and did not appear to be judgemental. I told them what I had done, of my own volition and things that I had been forced to do. Like the one time when I was ordered to execute a war captive in front of our entire military division. The commander was ruthless and wanted to see what the guys who were new in the division were made of. Me and two other guys were under his command for the very first time and I guess that we had to prove ourselves. We had taken over this little settlement that had put up some resistance. There were plenty of survivors. Men, women and children. The commander and his closest soldiers were probably salivating over the poor women. The men were criminals who opposed the caliphate, the judgement against them had been passed the moment they fired the first bullet back at us. At that point, I had already started questioning what on earth we were doing. The full scam had not been revealed to me yet but I had started becoming uneasy about a whole lot of things that I had seen done in the name of Islam. I was full of doubts but also not really sure about what was what, too much had happened too fast after I touched down in the new state's territory. I was confused to the point that I couldn't discern right from wrong. I'm not saying that in order to make some sort of excuse. I take full responsibility for every single action that I did. When it came to the killing of that prisoner that one day though...I really didn't want to do it. Before that I had killed, but it was on the battlefield. It's not the same thing. This particular time they had these guys out there in only their underwear and three of us had to execute one each with our handguns. The two others obeyed the order that was given and shot their hostage to death in front of the rest of us. Then it was my turn. I had two choices: kill this guy and maybe earn the trust of this devilish commander or refuse and have the others kill him and then take care of me afterwards, since I would be considered a traitor. I raised the gun and placed the muzzle about four inches away from the bottom of his skull. I closed my eyes and whispered astaghfirullah, I seek God's forgiveness. I squeezed the trigger and the sound of the gun going off was the loudest I had ever heard, and I had been next to grenades exploding and missiles striking down close to me. Nothing equaled the sound that the gun made on that occasion. He fell down in a heap, as if he was a sack of rice that had been dropped. The others exclaimed praises of God while I cursed them under my breath. It was perhaps my lowest point.

Ali did not flinch as I told him this story and other stories that I will leave out for the sake of brevity, but many of which are almost just as reprehensible. I was not the first of my kind that Ali had dealt with. He knew about these types of stories already, I was just a new face narrating them. I knew what I had done was wrong, my soul was telling me this. Ali then explained how it was empirically wrong according to the Islamic scholastic tradition. Example after example that I brought up of things that they had taught us as religious principles that we had to follow in order to be accepted as Muslims by Allah were shot down by Ali. The war that the "caliphate" was conducting, specially against other Muslims, the reinstitution of slavery and the taking of concubines, the suicide bombing missions, the way they performed the punishments and the way they judged "criminals" in the society, the pacts they had broken and a list of other things too long to enumerate here. He didn't only shoot them down, he disproved them with Quranic verses and prophetic hadiths. The same thing that Taymour had done to indoctrinate me, Ali was doing in reverse in order to pull me out of the swamp of extremism that I had got stuck in. It started clicking. Every verse he read and every hadith he quoted made my mind clearer and slowly peeled away the many layers of darkness that was wrapped around my heart.

It was not just him refuting the ideas that I had been taught and believed. My belief in them had become weaker and weaker for each atrocity that I had witnessed my companions commit in the name of Islam, but the core belief itself was never eradicated since I didn't have a counter narrative to replace it. Ali was the one that unlocked that door for me and he also made me see other things. He taught me much about what had happened to the local population and their sufferings. Let me tell you that story tomorrow if there is still life then. It is getting very late over here.

Our paranoid companion is going out on a reconnaissance mission apparently. He is still convinced that he had been spotted and will go out and see if he can figure out an escape plan from this place we are currently in. The other guy is telling him that it is too risky to go out and that we should rather lay as low as possible and hope that if the enemy is out there, they will think that the house we are in is uninhabited. The paranoid one won't take no for an answer on this one and seems determined to go out and check the surroundings in order to come up with the next gameplan. I'm content with writing as much as possible and letting destiny reveal itself as God wants it to. Hopefully I will talk to you tomorrow as well.

A. al-Naadim

October 25th

———

He came back in the middle of the night after being out for perhaps thirty to forty five minutes. He brought two things back with him: an escape plan and an intensified paranoia. The escape plan did not sound promising and was a sign of desperation. It entailed going back the same way that we had just come from and then veering off in a different direction, heading north, towards an area that is largely unknown to us but probably under the control of our enemies, who are hungry for revenge. Me and the other guy looked at each other with scepticism in our eyes as our companion relayed his plan. Our unconvinced expressions did not restrain his determination as he made it clear that we had to make a break for it this upcoming night, it was our last chance. I thought; sure why not. It was doom either way.

He was even more paranoid after this last tour outside the house than after the first one the day before. He had been spotted again, of course he had. He was even more certain this time. Several pairs of eyes had spotted him as he headed out and had also observed him as he made his way back. It almost sounded as if he wanted to make a run for it in broad daylight, but even the most desperate would have to admit that that would equal certain death. As soon as it becomes dark tonight we will pray the evening prayer, supplicate in hopes of receiving divine protection and then head out. That is the plan according to him and it is non-negotiable. Sure, whatever. At this point I have given up and I have understood a long time ago that it is a question of time. You might wonder why, if I have given up, I'm still connected to these guys and haven't tried to separate myself from them. There is only one thing that is holding me back from speeding the whole process up. Death is around the corner and has been for a while now. I could end the suffering if it wasn't for my very last mission, which is to finish telling my story and if I don't finish it I am at least making my best effort to tell as much of it as possible for the benefit of any potential readers. If no one reads it, then at least Allah will know that I made my best effort to make some sort of difference and I hope that will be taken into consideration when He judges me.

My visits to Rashid continued everytime that I returned to the capital. Ali was there every time, waiting to listen to me and always ready to answer a plethora of questions. I started writing things down. Many of the points he made I was scared that I would forget. He handed me a few notebooks. Way more than what I needed to take down notes, perhaps he had a premonition. I would also use these notebooks (one of which I'm writing in right now) to write down different observations and thoughts that struck me from time to time. I also wrote down all the questions that came to mind when I was not around my newfound teacher, so that I could ask him next time we met. These notebooks have not left my side since the day he gave them to me.

Ali exposed a lot more of the hypocrisy of the leadership that I did not know about. I had learned about their two-faced nature by looking at what they did and how they acted. He told me about things that I had not been privy to and could never have imagined. Much of the oil that the caliphate had secured by conquering territories that were the home to major oil fields and which was supposedly used to stimulate the local economy for the benefit of the citizens, was actually sold to the Syrian government. I couldn't believe my ears. The same tyrannical government that was by consensus the worst of all the players of this bizarre game of war. The leadership of the caliphate saw nothing wrong in making them a business partner in this endeavor. Ali didn't have to tell me that the oil profits didn't trickle down to the needy in the streets, a blind man could see that. Having heard that, I was hardly surprised when he told me that this new pseudo-government was also involved in drug-smuggling. The end is what mattered apparently, the means be damned. That soldiers were using was already known to me. I had seen soldiers fill themselves up with cocktails of pills before a battle and I had been offered pills myself on a few occasions. I always declined, pills were never my thing. There was a demand for them within the caliphate's own ranks and they had laid claim to many of the major transport routes in the region, so smuggling itself was not strange. The strange thing was that people who were self-proclaimed puritans were consuming them.

Ali told me that I should not be surprised, he had seen it many times before. People claimed to be religious in order to gain a following, then they restricted their religiosity in such a way that things could be excluded that would give them some personal benefit. Every single interpretation that could be made, no matter how far-fetched, would be made to serve one's own interests.

The thing that threw me off as much as anything else was our opponents in this war. Before I came here I was of the mind that we would be fighting imperialist forces and the oppressive regime of Syria, led by their devil of a president. We fought the regime's forces several times, that part held up, but I never saw any Western powers across from our barrels. I saw a bunch of troops that *supposedly* were allied with them but in my eyes they looked just like the regular Muslims in the area we lived in. That the leadership was saying that they were allied with America or Iran or whatever meant less and less after each battle. Most of the people we fought were Muslims. Many of them were Shia Muslims, which Taymour had declared early on was one of the biggest devils, but many others were people who identified themselves as Sunni Muslims. Which we did ourselves. So we were Sunnis fighting Sunnis, Muslims fighting Muslims. The whole idea of excommunicating these others and labeling them ipso facto apostates and unbelievers for rejecting the project of the caliphate started making sense after a while. It was the only way to justify fighting against them and taking their land. All with the hidden purpose of gaining power, wealth and influence. It had absolutely nothing to do with establishing justice, and there I was in the middle of it all burdened by being culpable.

The absurdity of it all was slowly revealing itself with each battle and after each talk I had with Ali. Imagine that I would have these talks with Ali, leaving each one a little more knowledgeable and with more disgust for the group I was a part of and then had to head back out into the battlefield. I'll share a short story, this was not that many weeks ago. At that point I was already all the way out. On the outside I pretended to be one of them in order to not be killed as an apostate, just like I am now, while being outraged on the inside and repulsed by everything that is going on and the things I'm taking part in. We are out fighting this Shia militia and actually defeated them (victories have been hard to come by lately) and we take a few captives. They didn't have any information that was valuable to us so the commander of our unit ordered us to execute the survivors. He handed a few of us one prisoner each and told us to go out from the camp and execute our respective prisoners somewhere far away as they were about to prepare dinner in the makeshift camp. I'm handed this guy who looks like he can hardly grow hairs on his chin. We all take our prisoner and start walking in different directions out from the camp. I don't want to kill this guy, he hasn't done anything to me personally and I hate everything about the caliphate. I'm just following orders in order to extend my own lifespan. As we are walking I start talking to him as tears are running down his cheeks and I can feel him trembling. I ask him about how he ended up in this mess. He told me he was an immigrant from Afghanistan that was fighting for Iran. He had been recruited with the promise that his family would receive residency in Iran if he joined this proxy army that he was in. The guy was only nineteen years old but looked closer to fifteen, perhaps his development stunted by conditions in his wartorn native land. He had been given a month of training before being sent out to the killing fields with the promise that his family would receive pension as compensation if he was killed in action. There were apparently soldiers even younger than him doing the same type of work. According to him, boys as young as sixteen were taking on the same role as him, the only difference was that they needed their parents' permission to join the war. I could see that he was here out of pure desperation. Nowhere in my soul could I find justification for killing this boy. In the distance we heard shots being fired in irregular intervals. I opened up the tie-wrap that had his hands tied up behind his back. He dropped to his knees. I told him to get up. At that point he wasn't just crying, rather floods were emanating from his eyes. I told him to shut up as his crying was getting louder and louder. Then I raised my weapon and told him: "See those hills over there? Make a run for them. Do your best to survive and whatever you do, don't come running back this way. Because if the people I'm with see you, they will kill us both."

He looked at me like he couldn't believe what he was hearing. His pants were dark down both legs from pissing himself. I told him one more time: "Save yourself and head for those hills. Now!" Then I fired off two shots towards the sky, just in case someone at the camp was keeping count of the shots fired out in the desert. He ran like I have never seen a human run before until he was no longer visible after disappearing behind the distant hills. I returned to camp hoping that the boy wouldn't cross our path in any way. He never did. We finished that campaign and headed back to the capital in order to regroup. On rare occasions we would go straight from one battlefront to another without going back home to recover. Standard procedure was to go back to the capital, a city that was more torn down every time I returned to it. On each short visit I would maximize my time with Ali and Rashid in hopes of gaining more knowledge and a better understanding of the situation. I was still, only a few weeks ago, still hoping that there would be some way out of this. I was hoping for an escape plan that would seem feasible, enough soldiers that gave up at the same time and changed sides, some miracle revealing itself that I could take advantage of. It never did. I fought a few more short battles. Incredibly enough I was spared from any severe injury. I have had a lot of bruises and serious cuts. I have caught shrapnel in both my legs and my ass. Bullets have grazed both my arms while only injuring me minimally. My hearing is really bad these days and I'm dealing with tinnitus. All things considered, I have made out fine. First of all, I'm still alive and I have all my limbs intact and my internal organs are all functioning. Most people that have been here for as long as I have can't make the same claim. I'm thankful for having been spared of the agony that a severe injury entails.

At the same time, it is the thing that forced me back into battle time and again. There was no form of disability that I had that could give me a dispensation. Then, a couple of weeks ago we were called upon to head out in a south eastern direction. There was a town that had rebelled. We had conquered it a good while back (by *we* I mean the caliphate, I wasn't part of that offensive). Now they had apparently raised up in rebellion so we were ordered to head over there and subdue the rebels. Little did we know that we walked straight into an ambush. The settlement had made a pact, unbeknownst to us, with a few of the surrounding groups, including a few Kurdish militias. We thought, blinded by our usual hubris, that we could roll in there and just handle business like we usually did with smaller foes. Before we knew it we were surrounded and they opened fire on us from all types of angles. They did it too early though, with more patience they would have wiped out our entire platoon. It led to a mad scramble in a chaotic environment and for a while it was every man for himself. Many on our side died instantaneously. They were lighting us up with automatic machine guns and rocket launchers. I saw a few in my platoon die right in front of my eyes as they were struck fatally. A few of us managed to find cover and a long firefight ensued. We recognized pretty fast that the position we held was not sustainable. We would have to split up in order to maximize the probability of a few of us surviving. We managed to hold them off for a few hours, one of our guys got killed during that time and another suffered an injury to the chest that would leave him more or less immobile. Saving him was not an option if we ourselves wanted to prolong our lives, so he was left behind soon thereafter.

The sun finally set. They thought they had us surrounded and they basically did, but they had holes in the ranks. We split up into four little groups, each determined to make it out. We made a run for it when darkness had engulfed the area. The opponents tried to light it up with the lights on their vehicles but there were still pockets of complete darkness here and there. As we tried to escape we heards shots going off followed by screams. Many fell during the escape. I don't know how many but I'm assuming the majority. There were four of us in my little group and it was the three that you know about that managed to get out from the trap that the enemy had lured us into. One guy got killed, simple math. We made it out and somehow managed to travel during that night without being detected. I have no idea how the other groups of escapees did and if anyone from any of those groups is still alive. Ever since that escape we have been surviving in the manner that I have been describing the last few weeks.

There are still so many things that I have to tell you. My conscience is far from clear. I still have many experiences to share with you that could possibly stop people from being recruited, that live in similar conditions to the ones I lived in when I fell for this enormous lie. I'm convinced that if we don't shed light on the reasons why these types of hateful messages become attractive to potential recruits, then we will never be able stop this phenomenon. Firstly, I have to te

That was the way the last diary entry ended. The last letter was written towards the bottom of the page with plenty of space left for more. There were several pages left in the notebook, over twenty of them, so it was not a matter of running out of paper to write on. It ended very abruptly, which might be fitting for something being written in an area where things change fast and under circumstances that were constantly unpredictable.

I hope that I throughout the text have been truthful to the original text and that the minute changes I have made for grammatical and cosmetic purposes don't in any way distort the intended meaning and ethos that the author wanted to present. I want to reiterate what I wrote in the introduction, many things the author writes I don't condone and a few of them I don't even feel are fit to print. Having said that, I feel it is my duty as an honest journalist that strives for integrity to publish his story without tampering with it. After all, it is his story and not mine. I'm only conveying it, and the positives that can be extracted from his story outweigh the negatives by far, in my opinion.

I also truly hope that it will one day reach the primary intended recipients, his family. My wish is also that it will have a positive impact on his target audience, youth that are grappling with the question of identity who are experiencing oppression in different forms and for different reasons. If this project I have undertaken can affect only one life and make that person change his or her course from one of destruction to one of positive productivity, then all the hours spent on this will be well worth it.